ANCHOR IN THE SEA

anchor

IN THE SEA

AN ANTHOLOGY OF PSYCHOLOGICAL FICTION

Edited by ALAN SWALLOW

THE SWALLOW PRESS and

WILLIAM MORROW & COMPANY, New York, 1947

PRINTED IN THE
UNITED STATES OF AMERICA

preface

One of the realms of realism in fiction is that of psychological phenomena—that realm in which one becomes aware of himself in the world about him. It is in that realm that one lives many of his critical moments, that he prepares the attitudes and decisions with which he acts in the public scene.

The development of this fiction, except possibly for stream-of-consciousness fiction, has been less spectacular in a public sense than the development of other varieties of contemporary realism. The story or the novel which grips closely the overt social problems of our day, and especially that story or novel which protests a deeply felt wrong in our society, has more readily gained response in the public imagination. Even stream-of-consciousness, although in an obvious sense "psychological," is but the other side of this coin, a study of the impact of a culture upon a consciousness which shows a minimum of direction or shaping. It has been remarked by critics that

James Joyce's *Ulysses* is a tremendous indictment of our culture. Like the contemporary poem, however, the psychological story most often seems to deal with private experience with subtlety, with concentration, and sometimes with private symbolism; the general response to this fiction is also analogous to the response to poetry.

Like the poem, again, the psychological story is frequently experimental, displaying a similar urge of the writer to find techniques with which to extend perception of the realities of the conscious life. In the following group of stories will be found, for example, the careful symbolism of title, as in such stories as "The Imaginary Jew" and "The Snowfall"; recurrent symbolism of object, as in "A Reunion"; symbolism of allusion, as in "Persephone"; hallucination of the dream-movie in "In Dreams Begin Responsibilities" or of conscious sensory awareness, as in "The Brink of Darkness." In making the following selections, I have not attempted a canvas of experimental techniques; yet many are represented in the stories. Most important, any experimental methods used in the stories gain for us, I am sure, not only a new, fresh perception but also a perception which is patterned within the story, is controlled in the sense that it is a valid judgment in human sensibility.

The close-knit, symbolical, and experimental nature of this fiction frequently relegates it to publication in the smaller circulation magazines. In studying these magazines for a number of years, I have been becoming more and more aware of the interest in this fiction among the most consciously critical of the editors of these magazines. Confident in the oblique support of my interest in this fiction by these editors, I have wanted to select an anthology which would show examples of this work alone. The result is a collection in which the short stories have all appeared in one or another of the small circulation magazines and which have had reprinting, if at all, only in books of comparatively small circulation. The fine short novel by Janet Lewis has had an analogous publishing history in that it first appeared from a comparatively small press.

Acknowledgment is gratefully made to the following for permission to use the materials of this volume:

To John Berryman and to the editors of *The Kenyon Review* for "The Imaginary Jew," the magazine's prize story for the year 1945.

To Kay Boyle and to the editors of *Accent* for "Wanderer."

To David Cornel DeJong and to the editors of *Southernesque* for "Preparations for the Night."

To Jean Garrigue and to the editors of *The Kenyon Review* for "The Snowfall," the magazine's prize story for the year 1944.

To Delmore Schwartz and to New Directions for "In Dreams Begin Responsibilities" from the volume entitled *In Dreams Begin Responsibilities* (Norfolk, Conn.: New Directions, 1938). This story originally appeared in *Partisan Review*.

To Jean Stafford and to the editors of *Partisan Review* for "A Reunion."

To Meridel Le Sueur and to the editors of *The Dial* for "Persephone."

To Kathleen Toole and to the editors of *The New Mexico Quarterly Review* for "A Short Space."

To Jessamyn West and to the editors of *The New Mexico Quarterly Review* for "The Child's Day."

To Yvor Winters and to the editors of *The Hound and Horn* for "The Brink of Darkness."

To Janet Lewis and to The Colt Press for *The Wife of Martin Guerre* (San Francisco: The Colt Press, 1941).

ALAN SWALLOW

The University of Denver
July 11, 1946

CONTENTS

JOHN BERRYMAN

the imaginary jew

THE SECOND summer of the European War I spent in New York. I lived in a room just below street-level on Lexington above 34th, wrote a good deal, tried not to think about Europe, and listened to music on a small gramophone, the only thing of my own, except books, in the room. Haydn's London Symphony, his last, I heard probably fifty times in two months. One night when excited I dropped the pickup, creating a series of knocks at the beginning of the last movement where the oboe joins the strings which still, when I hear them, bring up for me my low dark long damp room and I feel the dew of heat and smell the rented upholstery. I was trying, as one says, to come back a little, uncertain and low after an exhausting year. Why I decided to do this in New York—the enemy in summer equally of soul and body, as I had known for years—I can't remember; perhaps I didn't, but was held on merely from week to week by the motive which presently appeared in the form of a young woman met the Christmas before and now the occupation of every evening not passed in solitary and restless gloom. My friends were away; I saw few other people. Now and then I went to the zoo in lower Central Park and watched with interest the extraordinary behavior of a female badger. For a certain time she quickly paced the round of her cage. Then she would approach the sidewall from an angle in a determined, hardly perceptible, unhurried trot; suddenly, when an inch away, point her nose up it, follow her nose up over her back, turning a deft and easy somersault, from which she emerged on her feet moving swiftly and unconcernedly away, as if the action had been no affair of hers, indeed she had scarcely been present. There was another badger in the cage who never did this, and nothing else about her was remarkable; but this competent disinterested somersault she enacted once every five or ten minutes as long as I watched her,—quitting the wall, by the way, always at an angle in fixed relation to the angle at which she arrived at it. It is no longer possible to experience the pleasure I knew each time she lifted her nose and I understood again that she would not fail me, or feel the mystery of her absolute disclaimer,—she has been taken away or died.

The story I have to tell is no further a part of that special summer than a nightmare takes its character, for memory, from the phase of the moon one noticed on going to bed. It could have happened in another year and in another place. No doubt it did, has done, will do. Still, so weak is the talent of the mind for pure relation—immaculate apprehension of *p* alone—that everything helps us, as when we come to an unknown city: architecture, history, trade-practices, folklore. Even more anxious our approach to a city—like my small story—which we have known and forgotten. Yet how little we can learn! Some of the history is the lonely summer. Part of the folklore, I suppose, is what I now unwillingly rehearse, the character which experience has given to my sense of the Jewish people.

Born in a part of the South where no Jews had come, or none had stayed, and educated thereafter in States where they are numerous, I somehow arrived at a metropolitan university without any clear idea of what in modern life a Jew was,—without even a clear consciousness of having seen one. I am unable now to explain this simplicity or blindness. I had not escaped, of course, a sense that humans somewhat different from ourselves, called "Jews," existed as in the middle distance and were best kept there, but this sense was of the vaguest. From what it was derived I do not know; I do not recall feeling the least curiosity about it, or about Jews; I had, simply, from the atmosphere of an advanced heterogeneous democratic society, ingathered a gently negative attitude towards Jews. This I took with me, untested, to college, where it received neither confirmation nor stimulus for two months. I rowed and danced and cut classes and was political; by mid-November I knew most of the five hundred men in my year. Then the man who rowed Number Three, in the eight of which I was bow, took me aside in the shower one afternoon and warned me not to be so chatty with Rosenblum.

I wondered why not. Rosenblum was stroke, a large handsome amiable fellow, for whose ability in the shell I felt great respect and no doubt envy. Because the fellows in the House wouldn't like it, my friend said. "What have they against him?" "It's only because he's Jewish," explained my friend, a second-generation Middle European.

I hooted at him, making the current noises of disbelief, and went back under the shower. It did not occur to me that he could be right. But next day when I was talking with Herz, the coxswain, whom I knew very well, I remembered the libel with some annoyance, and told Herz about it as a curiosity. Herz looked at me oddly, lowering his head, and said after a pause, "Why, Al *is* Jewish, didn't you know that?" I was amazed. I said it was absurd, he couldn't be! "Why not?" said Herz, who must have been as astonished as I was. "Don't you know I'm Jewish?"

I did not know, of course, and ignorance has seldom cost me such humiliation. Herz did not guy me; he went off. But greater than my shame at not knowing something known, apparently, without effort to everyone else, were my emotions for what I then quickly discovered. Asking careful questions during the next week, I learnt that about a third of the men I spent time with in college were Jewish; that they knew it, and the others knew it; that some of the others disliked them for it, and they knew this also; that certain Houses existed *only* for Jews, who were excluded from the rest; and that what in short I took to be an idiotic state was deeply established, familiar, and acceptable to everyone. This discovery was the beginning of my instruction in social life proper—construing social life as that from which political life issues like a somatic dream.

My attitude toward my friends did not alter on this revelation. I merely discarded the notion that Jews were a proper object for any special attitude; my old sense vanished. This was in 1933. Later, as word of the German persecution filtered into this country, some sentimentality undoubtedly corrupted my no-attitude. I denied the presence of obvious defects in particular Jews, feeling that to admit them would be to side with the sadists and murderers. Accident allotting me close friends who were Jewish, their disadvantages enraged me. Gradually, and against my sense of impartial justice, I became the anomaly which only a partial society can produce, and for which it has no name known to the lexicons. In one area, not exclusively, "nigger-lover" is flung in a proximate way: but for a special sympathy and liking for Jews—which became my fate, so that I trembled when I heard one abused in talk—we have no term. In this condition I still was during the summer of which I speak. One further circumstance may be mentioned, as a product, I believe, of this curious training. I am spectacularly unable to identify Jews as Jews,—by name, cast of feature, accent, or environment,—and this has been true, not only of course before the college incident, but during my whole life since. Even names to anyone else patently Hebraic rarely suggest to me anything. And when once I learn that So-and-so is Jewish, I am likely to forget it. Now Jewishness—the religion or the race—may be a fact as striking and informative as someone's past heroism or his Christianity or his understanding of the subtlest human relations, and I feel sure that something operates to prevent my utilizing the plain signs by which such characters—in a Jewish man or woman—may be identified, and prevent my retaining the identification once it is made.

So to the city my summer and a night in August. I used

to stop on Fourteenth Street for iced coffee, walking from the Village home (or to my room rather) after leaving my friend, and one night when I came out I wandered across to the island of trees and grass and concrete walks raised in the center of Union Square. Here men—a few women, old—sit in the evenings of summer, looking at papers or staring off or talking, and knots of them stay on, arguing, very late; these the unemployed or unemployable, the sleepless, the malcontent. There are no formal orators, as at Columbus Circle in the nineteen-thirties and at Hyde Park Corner. Each group is dominated by several articulate and strong-lunged persons who battle each other with prejudices and desires, swaying with intensity, and take on from time to time the interrupters: a forum at the bottom of the pot,—Jefferson's fear, Whitman's hope, the dream of the younger Lenin. It was now about one o'clock, almost hot, and many men were still out. I stared for a little at the equestrian statue, obscure in the night on top of its pedestal, thinking that the misty Rider would sweep again away all these men at his feet, whenever he liked,—what symbol for power yet in a mechanical age rivals the mounted man?—and moved to the nearest group; or I plunged to it.

The dictator to the group was old, with dark cracked skin, fixed eyes in an excited face, leaning forward madly on his bench towards the half-dozen men in semicircle before him. "It's bread! it's bread!" he was saying. "It's bitter-sweet. All the bitter and all the sweetness. Of an overture. What else do you want? When you ask for steak and potatoes, do you want pastry with it? It's bread! It's bread! Help yourself! Help yourself!"

The listeners stood expressionless, except one who was smiling with contempt and interrupted now.

"Never a happy minute, never a happy minute!" the old man cried. "It's good to be dead! Some men should kill themselves."

"Don't you want to live?" said the smiling man.

"Of course I want to live. Everyone wants to live! If death comes, suddenly it's better. It's better!"

With pain I turned away. The next group were talking diffusely and angrily about the Mayor, and I passed to a third, where a frantic olive-skinned young man with a fringe of silky beard was exclaiming:

"No restaurant in New York had the Last Supper! No. When people sit down to eat they should think of that!"

"Listen," said a white-shirted student on the rail, glancing around for approbation, "listen, if I open a restaurant and put *The Last Supper* up over the door, how much money do you think I'd lose? Ten thousand dollars?"

The fourth cluster was larger and appeared more coherent. A savage argument was in progress between a man of fifty with an oily red face, hatted, very determined in manner, and a muscular fellow half his age with heavy eyebrows, coatless, plainly Irish. Fifteen or twenty men were packed around them, and others on a bench near the rail against which the Irishman was lounging were attending also. I listened for a few minutes. The question was whether the President was trying to get us into the War,—or rather, whether this was legitimate, since the Irishman claimed that Roosevelt was a goddamned warmonger whom all the real people in the country hated, and the older man claimed that we should have gone into the f–ing war when France fell a year before, as everybody in the country knew except a few immigrant rats. Redface talked ten times as much as the Irishman, but he was not able to establish any advantage that I could see. He ranted, and then Irish either repeated shortly and fiercely what he had said last, or shifted his ground. The audience were silent–favoring whom I don't know, but evidently much interested. One or two men pushed out of the group, others arrived behind me, and I was eddied forward towards the disputants. The young Irishman broke suddenly into a tirade by the man with the hat:

"You're full of s. Roosevelt even tried to get us in with the communists in the Spanish war. If he could have done it we'd have been burning churches down like the rest of the Reds."

"No, that's not right," I heard my own voice, and pushed forward, feeling blood in my face, beginning to tremble. "No, Roosevelt as a matter of fact helped Franco by non-intervention, at the same time that Italians and German planes were fighting against the Government and arms couldn't get in from France."

"What's that? What are you, a Jew?" He turned to me contemptuously, and was back at the older man before I could speak. "The only reason we weren't over there four years ago is because you can only screw us so much. Then we quit. No New Deal bastard could make us go help the goddamned communists."

"That ain't the question, it's if we want to fight *now* or *later*. Them Nazis ain't gonna sit!" shouted the redfaced man. "They got Egypt practically, and then it's India if it ain't England first. It ain't a question of the communists, the communists are on Hitler's side. I tellya we can wait and wait and chew and spit and the first thing you know they'll be in England, and then who's gonna help us when they start after us? Maybe Brazil? Get wise to the world! Spain don't matter now one way or the other, they ain't gonna help and they can't hurt. It's Germany and Italy and Japan, and if it ain't too late now it's gonna be. Get wise to yourself. We shoulda gone in—"

"What with?" said the Irishman with disdain. "Pop pop. Wooden machine-guns?"

"We were as ready a year ago as we are now. Defense don't mean nothing, you gotta have to fight!"

"No, we're much better off now," I said, "than we were a year ago. When England went in, to keep its word to Poland, what good was it to Poland? The German Army—"

"Shut up, you Jew," said the Irishman.

"I'm not a Jew," I said to him. "What makes—"

"Listen, Pop," he said to the man in the hat, "it's O.K. to shoot your mouth off, but what the hell have you got to do with it? You aren't gonna do any fighting."

"Listen," I said.

"You sit on your big ass and talk about who's gonna fight who. Nobody's gonna fight anybody. If we feel hot, we ought to clean up some of the sons of bitches here before we go sticking our nuts anywhere to help England. We ought to clean up the sons of bitches in Wall Street and Washington before we take any ocean trips. You want to know something? You know why Germany's winning everything in this war? Because there ain't no Jews back home. There ain't no more Jews, first shouting war like this one here"—nodding at me—"and then skinning off to the synagogue with the profits. Wake up, Pop! You must have been around in the last war, you ought to know better."

I was too nervous to be angry or resentful. But I began to have a sense of oppression in breathing. I took the Irishman by the arm.

"Listen, I told you I'm not a Jew."

"I don't give a damn what you are." He turned his half-dark eyes to me, wrenching his arm loose. "You talk like a Jew."

"What does that mean?" Some part of me wanted to laugh. "How does a Jew talk?"

"They talk like you, buddy."

"That's a fine argument! But if I'm not a Jew, my talk only—"

"You probably are a Jew. You look like a Jew."

"I *look* like a Jew? Listen"—I swung around with despair to a man standing next to me—"do I look like a Jew? It doesn't matter whether I do or not—a Jew is as good as anybody and better than this son of a bitch." I was not exactly excited, I was trying to adapt my language as my need for the crowd, and sudden respect for its judgment, possessed me. "But in fact I'm not Jewish and I don't look Jewish. Do I?"

The man looked at me quickly and said, half to me and half to the Irishman, "Hell, I don't know. Sure he does."

A wave of disappointment and outrage swept me almost to tears. I felt like a man betrayed by his brother. The lamps seemed brighter and vaguer, the night large. Glancing round I saw sitting on a bench near me a tall, heavy, serious-looking man of thirty, well dressed, whom I had noticed earlier, and appealed to him, "Tell me, do I look Jewish?"

But he only stared up and waved his head vaguely. I saw with horror that something was wrong with him.

"You look like a Jew. You talk like a Jew. You *are* a Jew," I heard the Irishman say.

I heard murmuring among the men, but I could see nothing very clearly. It seemed very hot. I faced the Irishman again helplessly, holding my voice from rising.

"I'm *not* a Jew," I told him. "I might be, but I'm not. You have no bloody reason to think so, and you can't make me a Jew by simply repeating like an idiot that I am."

"Don't deny it, son," said the redfaced man, "stand up to him."

"God damn it"—suddenly I was furious, whirling like a fool (was I afraid of the Irishman? had he conquered me?) on the redfaced man—"I'm *not* denying it! Or rather I am, but only because I'm not a Jew! I despise renegades, I hate Jews who turn on their people, if I were a Jew I would say so, I would be proud to be: what is the vicious opinion of a man like this to me if I were a Jew? But I'm not. Why the hell should I admit I am if I'm not?"

"Jesus, the Jew is excited," said the Irishman.

"I have a right to be excited, you son of a bitch. Suppose I call you a Jew. Yes, you're a Jew. Does that mean anything?"

"Not a damn thing." He spat over the rail past a man's head.

"Prove that you're not. I say you are."

"Now listen, you Jew. I'm a Catholic."

"So am I, or I was born one, I'm not one now. I was born a Catholic." I was a little calmer but goaded, obsessed with the need to straighten this out. I felt that everything for everyone there depended on my proving him wrong. If *once* this evil for which we have not even a name could be exposed to the rest of the men as empty—if I could *prove* I was not a Jew—it would fall to the ground, neither would anyone else be a Jew to be accused. Then it could be trampled on. Fascist America was at stake. I listened, intensely anxious for our fate.

"Yeah?" said the Irishman. "Say the Apostles' Creed."

Memory went swirling back. I could hear the little bell die as I hushed it and set it on the felt. Father Boniface looked at me tall from the top of the steps and smiled greeting me in the darkness before dawn as I came to serve, the men pressed around me under the lamps, and I could remember nothing but *visibilum omnium* . . . et invisibilium?

"I don't remember it."

The Irishman laughed with his certainty.

The papers in my pocket; I thought them over hurriedly. In my wallet. What would they prove? Details of ritual, Church history: anyone could learn them. My piece of Irish blood. Shame, shame: shame for my ruthless people. I will not be his blood. I wish I were a Jew, I would change my blood, to be able to say *Yes* and defy him.

"I'm not a Jew." I felt a fool. "You only say so. You haven't any evidence in the world."

He leaned forward from the rail, close to me. "Are you cut?"

Shock, fear ran through me before I could make any

meaning out of his words. Then they ran faster, and I felt confused.

From that point, nothing is clear for me. I stayed a long time—it seemed impossible to leave, showing him victor to them—thinking of possible allies and new plans of proof, but without hope. I was tired to the marrow. The arguments rushed on, and I spoke often now but seldom was heeded except by an old fat woman, very short and dirty, who listened intently to everyone. Heavier and heavier appeared to me to press upon us in the fading night our general guilt.

In the days following, as my resentment died, I saw that I had not been a victim altogether unjustly. My persecutors were right: I was a Jew. The imaginary Jew I was was as real as the imaginary Jew hunted down, on other nights and days, in a real Jew. Every murderer strikes the mirror, the lash of the torturer falls on the mirror and cuts the real image, and the real and the imaginary blood flow down together.

KAY BOYLE

wanderer

To Pegeen Vail

He had come to this part of the French Alps in August, or perhaps the end of July it was, and rented a ground-floor room with a balcony to it in the house just down the road: a man of thirty or thereabouts with dark hair and white teeth and an opera singer's loud agnostic laugh. He was not a very tall man, but his shoulders were broad and his waist thin, and he had scars in his cheeks when he smiled and even when he didn't, as if in the country he came from that was the way a man vindicated his own or a woman's honor. It was easy enough to think of him in fencer's tights and a neat-wristed blouse dancing nimbly this way and that on the balls of his feet, the rapier poised for thrust or defense, and the eyes ready, black, and quick as a Spaniard's might have been but not like an Italian's or an Oriental's indolent eyes.

It was Judith (fourteen years and a few months more that summer) who first saw him coming up the road or down it, sometimes dressed in linen slacks with a racquet under his arm on his way to the hotel for tennis, and sometimes dressed in corduroys with a knapsack on his shoulders, prepared for climbing higher. And whenever he passed the Americans' châlet he lifted his eyes and looked at it; he glanced up at the sloping alpine roof, and the balconies, and briefly but tensely at the windows—perhaps as impersonally as if he were looking merely at Mont-Blanc beyond them, but looking just the same. Standing a little to one side of the glass so that the daylight could not pick her out, Judith could see the way the hair grew back from the point on his brow, and the sunburned flesh, and the nostril's flare; could come to the window day after day and wait unseen for the black sardonic eye and the dark lip's curve and the shoulders' breadth descending, or see the narrow hips and the bowed black head climbing the other way. Once or twice mother, passing through the room, paused to look out without wonder on the bronzed hands and throat and the clefted chin, and the firm easy gait of a man who knows exactly where he's going, and how high the mountain is, and how deep the river, and how long it will take him, whatever obstacles race and nationality and man's intolerance might put before him, to reach the place to which he is destined to go.

"He looks a bit like a waiter," mother said, smoking her cigarette behind the pane. "I can just see him coming into a restaurant with a tray balanced on one hand, and perhaps even spilling a little of the soup. . . ."

"A waiter!" breathed Judith, standing just out of sight with her hair as light as taffy, and her face small, and her legs long as a foal's. "Oh, mother, not a waiter—!" While her heart said in silence: Oh, spare me, spare me, if he lifts his eyes again and looks this way!

Nobody knew his name or where he had come from, but Judith had endowed him with a history as grim as Heathcliff's own. She would shut the door of her room at night and do her teeth and comb her fair hair out, and then she would sit a long time copying the words about him into the leather-backed book, her head hanging delicate as a flower into the lamp's pure cone of light.

"He is a dark-skinned gypsy in aspect," she wrote, taking it carefully from page three, paragraph two, and leaving out the words that did not apply. "In dress and manners a gentleman . . . I know, by instinct, his reserve springs from an aversion to showy displays of feeling—to manifestations of human kindliness. He'll love and hate equally under cover, and esteem it a species of impertinence to be loved or hated again."

For twice she had heard the wild cinematic wind howl down the moors, and watched the simulated rains drench in sad poetic fury over Hollywood's Thrushcross Grange and the Blackhorse marsh to Wuthering Heights, weeping silently and savagely there in the French movie theater's velvet-covered fauteuil for Cathy's love and Heathcliff's inarticulate pain. For the ninth time she had reached page sixty-seven, paragraph six, and read in solemn anguish:

"I've dreamed in my life dreams that have stayed with me ever after . . . they've gone through and through me, like wine through water, and altered the color of my mind,"—while the dark man, the sleeves of his soft blue jersey knotted and clinging around his neck as the arms of a woman might, walked down the road to where his rented room was and closed the door upon his loneliness, and hope expired from the day.

Because it was August, the talk of Poland and what might be coming had already begun, but no one had thought to wonder about him yet or sought to endow him with a nationality. All that month he was simply the foreigner, free as any foreigner to come and rent a room for a few weeks in the mountains, and free to look as he looked at women, and free to lift his eyes to any window when he went past on the road. The day of the cattle fair fell on the twenty-seventh or eighth, and the sun still shone, and that was the third time Judith saw him close enough to touch him if she had stretched out her hand. He was leaning on the top bar of the fence they had set up for the occasion around the place where people skated in the wintertime, leaning there to watch the calves that had broken loose from their pens frolicking like young lambs in the dust of the square. He was wearing a blue shirt and his head was bare, and as he watched the calves playing the game of tag like children together, he threw his head back and laughed the mirthless, operatic laugh. Only when he saw Judith crossing from the shooting gallery did his mouth close suddenly, as if upon words he could not trust himself to say.

(The first time she had ever come close to him was in the evening, coming home from a music lesson in the mountain dusk; and in spite of the heart's trepidation she had dared to see the scars on his face, those engraved emblems of a man's repeated courage flaying, as if in cool white fury, the cheeks' dark sunburned flesh, and dared to meet the eyes' mysterious salutation. And the second time passed close to him when he stood beneath the cobbler's window where the statue of the Virgin Mary and the canary's cage were set out in the sun; saw him, in spite of the blinding, bewildering hand of timidity across her vision, standing with his head lifted and his throat bare in the shirt's open neck and the lips shaped to whistle the bird's notes clearly and truly up the house's wall to where it hung confined, the sound sweet and wondrous enough for man or child or bird to pause and listen.) But now when they passed each other near the merry-go-round on the cattle-packed square or halted by the tethered goats an instant, there was never a word to say to him, not even "bon jour" to give and take, only his eyes moving, dark and ardent, past mother's face to Judith's face.

Then on the second of September, this happened: the jointed pipe which drew the rain and in winter the melted snow down from the châlet's roof to the ground had come apart and Judith, gray slacks shielding the foal's young legs, was trying to shinny up it. She was trying to reach the break with one hand and fit it piece to piece again, holding hard with her knees and stretching high, when the voice spoke out behind her from the ground. It spoke in French, but with an accent to it, speaking bitterly but gently to her, and the silver bracelets clattered in terror down her arm.

"I could help you then, perhaps," it said. "I am taller, you see, so perhaps I could be the one to reach up there better."

The heart might then have ceased to function, the blood abruptly halted in its scheduled movement from vein to vein, the eyes at that instant been stricken blind, and the breath strangled in the throat—for, with the anguished music of the drowning playing in her ears, she slid down the pipe's funnel to the ground and stood there, not breathing yet and seeing nothing for a long time but the reeling wheels of sunlight while she rubbed the insides of her hands in slow senseless motion with her handkerchief's wadded ball. Before she could find the look or word to give him (if sound could possibly have been given tongue or eye the fearful power of sight), he had, in a single bound, achieved the summit of the garage door whose swinging panels folded inward and outward, outward and inward on their hinges like a paper screen. There he balanced without effort, sitting perilously on the narrow edge, his feet in the tennis shoes and the cuffs of the white knitted socks rolled at the ankles just even now with her eyes.

"I'm afraid the oil—that is to say, I think the oil we paint the wood with," she began saying, the French words stammered fast. "I mean, I'm afraid it comes off—it may come off on your clothes, that is—from the door, I mean—" And the dark man sitting perched on the fluctuating edge spoke down the distance to her, saying:

"You are kind to think of me, Mademoiselle, you are very kind to think of me. I have been a long time without anybody thinking about me that way," and he reached out for the two covered pieces of pipe along the châlet's wall.

While he worked, the garage door folded in and out, mercilessly in and out, with only the body's poise and weight saying in silence, quiet, quiet, and gently now, gently now, to it as the voice might cajole a fractious mount. She saw the pure white teeth bite down into the lip, and the soles of the canvas shoes press flat against the panels of the door, and the veins stand dark in his temples for a moment—the grudgingly given betrayals of the flesh's strain. In another minute he had fitted the pipe's joint into joint, and when it was done he leapt down to the ground and brushed his hands off, and the garage door clattered back upon itself in freedom and left them looking into each other's faces. And now the mouth that had shaped the notes of music for the bird and the Virgin, and the accompaniment of laughter for the calves gamboling on the square, said almost in shyness to her:

"It is this language I cannot speak very well. It is not my language and I have not been here such a long time to learn it," saying the French words in a way no Frenchman would have liked to hear them said. "Here I have not friends as I have in my own country," he said, "and I think without friends it is difficult to learn the words in any country, it is difficult even to live without a feeling that you are among them—I am trying to say this, that you are among friends even if the right words are not always found at once to be said to each other—"

"Yes," Judith whispered, looking in desperation at the little space of ground that lay between them. "Yes, I know."

"But you have learned to speak it," he said. "You are not French, of course, I saw for a long time that you are not French, and still you have learned to speak. You are English, are you? I have said every day, and I was very glad to say so, that you are an English girl." Before she could say no to it, say No, we're Americans, mother and father and I Americans, he went on saying: "I have an

English pound. I have one English pound sterling now in my room. When I was getting through Switzerland a friend gave it to me to help me when I needed it." She could feel the power of his eyes on her, moving over her hair and face in nameless emotion, and she could not bear to lift her own eyes and see the teeth white as a wolf's in the sunburned face, and the marks of valor scarring the cheeks, and the eyes hot and violent under the tilted black wings of the brows. "Perhaps your father would like the pound," he was saying. "The banks here will not change foreign money any longer. A little town is like that when they feel disaster is on the way. One day you could ask your father if he would like the pound," he said.

"Yes," said Judith, not daring to see his face still, and she clung for courage to the wadded handkerchief in her palms.

"And now perhaps the war coming, perhaps tomorrow, perhaps the next day," he went on, harshly and nervously. "The war coming along to prove this to everyone again—to prove to you and me and everyone that all languages are useless, all speech useless to everyone. All the small countries to be lost over again, and nations and races sent wandering although they haven't much wanderlust left in their blood any more. 'Thou shalt wander on the earth till I return,'" he said bitterly, "and so we wander—people without houses, without a homeland, without food even—"

Without looking up into his face, she knew suddenly that what he needed was the money, he needed the francs badly, needed to have them in his pocket that afternoon and tomorrow to carry him down into the village with him for the loaf of bread or the butter or eggs or the cheese he didn't have.

"How much does a pound make?" she said in a low, eager voice to him. "I mean, my father and mother aren't here today—but if you could tell me how many francs there are in a pound—I mean, you see, I have a little money but perhaps it wouldn't be enough money—"

"How much have you got?" the dark man said, and her heart repeated: "A half-civilized ferocity lurked yet in the depressed brows and eyes full of black fire, but it was subdued; and his manner was even dignified: quite divested of roughness, though too stern for grace."

"I have about two hundred and fifty francs," she said, the voice expiring, and the dark man said that would do.

That was the second of September, the day she broke the glazed swan on her desk open and gave him the money he said he had to have for the pound. The pound itself was locked away in his room and he said he would give it to her the next time he came up the road, and then he looked around quickly for a bit of wood and found it and stooped down and began drawing the lines out carefully on the earth. Now that his eyes were turned to something else, she could look at him; she could see how the hair grew on his head, black and neatly shaped and strong, and the thick dark fringe of lash along the eyelid, and the narrow wrist, and the sunburned hand with the stick held in it.

"Like that," he said, and she watched as if bewitched the side of his face and the way his lips moved. "This was the game we used to play. We played it every day after school with the girls in the park, going home under the trees, before we had time to forget the lessons they taught us—the philosophers' and the poets', even Schiller's *Freiheit in der Erscheinung* which has been blotted out as if it was a mistake on the page— And then we put numbers, you see," he went on saying, "different numbers inside each one, and then a little stone, like this, a pebble to knock along with the foot—"

"Hop-scotch," said Judith, and because his eyes were on her the color ran up her throat to the light line of her hair.

They played the jumping, one-legged game all that afternoon, first the dark man with the francs jumping in his pocket hopping and throwing his head back to laugh almost in delight when he didn't touch the lines; and then Judith hopping solemnly from square to designated square under the kitchen windows, the white rim of the eternally iced mountains all about them encircling the lower hills. And whether she had perceived them there when she came up from the village, or merely seen the record left in Judith's face, it was mother who cast the first stone at the stranger across the table that evening. She said:

"The baker-woman asked me today if I knew anything about that dark man who lives down the road, and I told her I didn't. She said people have seen him reading letters written in another language—German or Russian or something unfamiliar—"

"I wouldn't write a letter in any language for the next twenty-four hours, familiar or unfamiliar," father said, but he didn't look up from the copy of *Time* he was reading. He was trying to find out if there was going to be a war or if there wasn't and he didn't have a moment to spare.

Once in her room that night, Judith closed the door quickly, and caught her breath, and looked a long time at her face, at the front of it and the side of it, in the glass. War or the threat of war were nothing, and the broken swan with the money gone from it nothing, less than nothing, and without doing her teeth first she sat down in the lamplight at her desk and began copying the words out from page sixty-eight, with her hair falling bright gold across the open book.

"He shall never know how I love him," she wrote, "and that not because he's handsome but because he's more myself than I am. Whatever our souls are made of, his and mine are the same . . . My love for him resembles the eternal rocks beneath," with her finger running the length of each line to guide her eye to it.

The next day was Sunday, and she saw him sitting about midday on the café terrace underneath the trees, sitting with a glass of something cool before him just out of the dust that rose from under the wheels of the charabancs and the cars and buses hurrying through the village, and for an instant she thought of the pound note he hadn't given her yet, and then the thought ignited with shame and perished in her mind. He was sitting there alone with a newspaper open in the fingers of one hand, and he did not see her passing, for his head was dropped a little forward to read those words that traced the history of irretrievable steps up to the latest hour, the press not yet pronouncing the single syllable of final disaster loudly and clearly enough for everyone to hear. He sat there under the trees with his left hand up to his forehead, not looking at the men or the women or the cars passing, but looking in blind, quiet despair at what might have been the sight of the world, or at least his own world, falling bit by bit and irredeemably away.

On Monday he did not come up the road or down it, and Tuesday at lunch mother asked father what the exchange on pounds and francs was and, from behind the copy of *Life,* father said:

"It's just about what it's been for some time now. Around a hundred and seventy-five."

"Because that dark man down the road gave a pound note to the baker-woman," mother went on saying. "He didn't have the francs to pay the bill before he left, so he gave her that. She asked me how much it would make because the banks aren't giving any exchanges–"

"Before he left?" Judith said, putting her fork down. "Before he–" And suddenly the chairs swooned, and the table swung, and the windows in which the brilliant sun had stood were blotted out with dark.

"He went off last night. The baker-woman said he went off with the gendarmes," mother said, her voice hallooing to hearing across the vast terrible expanses of pain. "He's probably going to be interned for the–"

"Which dark man are you talking about?" said father, the words from behind the copy of *Life* as if called out in the hands' cupped megaphone from an incredibly safe, far shore.

"The one that looked like a waiter," mother said, and Judith stood up, swaying like the drunk, as the cortège of the dead went past her–Cathy's stabbed restless heart, and Heathcliff's eyes unclosing–and tried to walk towards the stairs.

DAVID CORNEL DE JONG

preparations for the night

SIMPLICITY. Everything reduced to a most intricate simplicity, ad absurdum. No thoughts left to call one's own; everything, thoughts and all, gone in the family wash. Not even one short line for one's familiar underdrawers, alone to flaunt one's own separateness! Part of the whole, the sweet whole, like brethren in one house, lovely like the oil dripping from Aaron's beard. "Now, when I was young . . ." They clatter the answer on it, like a lid on steam. "Ha!" they laughed at him. "When you were young, as if we don't know how to be young." Relegated ruthlessly to the old-man class; loose old horse-lips, drooling tobacco juice over dead gums with no teeth. Gibbering old wisdoms with intricate precision. Hobbling on old shoes from which the nails came and scratched the noise from the sidewalk right into the soul, right through your liver and kidneys—but hell, eighty per cent of all old men are deaf; they don't hear it.

He leaned back and tormented himself more; himself, the only one he was allowed to torment or to coddle. He looked at the fierce black wallpaper strangely shutting him in. Black teasels, black tendrils, black buds and gray wide blossoms against the murky gray of it all. Couldn't even see a fly make peregrinations along those jungle tendrils without losing him and making the eyes water. Again he rose, and with the blue pencil in his hand he traced blue circles around the gray wallpaper flowers. He traced seven of them this time. Which made, now let's see, eighteen and nine . . . "F'r God's sake cut that out!"—and yes, that last one she'd interrupted yesterday. He went and finished the half circle of that one, and set the rocker in front of it so that the shadow of one of the high knobs fell over it. "Now, when I was your age . . ."

He listened. All their voices a braiding of evil, a twisting of smallnesses, crullers of animosities, pretzels of banalities, twisting through each other, Medusa's snake-locks, twisting along in the world of space and matter and holiness. The radio, too. A conundrum. He was now bending his head toward the door, batting the eyelids furiously, hearing: "Oh, you go hang. You shut your big trap before somebody falls in it or you swallow the lamp. And you!" Oh, what the hell's the use? "When we were a couple of kids"—the last the radio, soprano above it all, demoniacal, should have the accompaniment of the vacuum cleaner or the chugging of the old water-power washing machine as obligato. "The hell with you. Other men can. Why can't you? Where's the damned kid? Where's that damned mush mouth?" "Look on the shelf, you big palooka."

Wonderful. He shut his eyes. Shut them so hard and so deep that they sank way inside of him, way down where his heart was. The eyes, sinking, sinking, sinking through the blue water coldness which was his heart, whence love used to come. Love seeped out through the cracked-red-valentine heart walls. But his eyes lay inside, so deep. He no longer heard the voices wheezing through the amber light bar under the door. Eyes drifting, sinking, touching bottom, coming up with nothing, not even one stringy seaweed of tender thinking. The thoughts and love rise from the heart for the choleric man, after that the wheel of fortune, the horoscope, finally after it all the phoenix standing hungry on its ashes, standing like a crow on dry beach sand in Florida. That was it when I was young. It was in the almanacs. "To hell, to hell, to hell, you say."

He sighed, opened his eyes frantically, and saw a fly go past a blue-limned gray blossom, travel on. He may reach another blossom so. Call that one Copenhagen. Lovely town. Call the fly the Lindberghs. He sat taut, pushing his hands wedge-wise between the narrow thighs, looking, looking, no longer seeing the fly because his looking had become an indefinite haze, a wallpaper blur, black tendrils strangling his looking into momentary forgetting. He cried a very little and listened again, hearing nothing, hearing so much, it was nothing but a vast agony, like the wallpaper, blurring into his thinking. And from there on they wandered into Mozambique, past rusty idols standing knee-deep in fireweeds, and the heralds shouted from the balconies. Trumpeted, rather. Wild peacock colorings on his thinking, opiates.

His eyes opened carefully again, no longer smarting and burning; his fingers tested the stubble on his chin. Would have to ask *him* to be shaved. Him with the beet face, mouth snapping every question in two, eyes like blue rabbit intestines, spoiled. Ask him, quaver the voice, first strains of the symphony, then the pause—muting of everything, everything bated in expectation—until the fanfare of answer and later his hard knotted hands like brick tongs twisting his old stiff neck so and so. Blessed are the poor for they shall inherit heaven. Blessed are they who suffer for . . .

He thought of his thinking, his fingers digging into the green bound book which was for morning sun hours, hopeless now, Tantalus. To think of one's thinking. Thinking what they beyond the door who never thought had done with his thinking. They, like big blue cold hands, twisting into the cup of his skull, grabbing at the convolutions of his brain, like the women at Lofoten—oh, ages ago, when I was very young, with a pair of brown corduroy pants that whistled like guinea pigs. Where was I? Yes, like the big Lofoten women, twisting with hard and dexterous hands, unsentimental, the slippery offal out of huge codfish, then the grubby knives, scraping against the bone, scraping now in his head, close to the skull, all threads and ligaments out of it, everything, and soon now the fat blue bottle flies would be over it in the reeking sun, and last, maggots. That's what they had done to his thinking.

They who now: "Oh, don't you just love Kate Smith? Don't you?" "You big fig, whynjesee where you step with those big clodhoppers? Whynjewear snow-shoes, anyway?" "Hell, you know those funny little jiggers? Get them with toothpaste free at the five and ten, like dentists use to look at the backyard of your teeth. Sure. Makes your tooth look like a garage. Wouldn't that make you scream? Tooth like a garage." Oh, shut up. "Mama! Yippy's got his pants unbuttoned. Ma-a-a! Look at Yippy will ye?" "Now the Hitler régime can lead to nothing but barbarism, relapse." That latter the radio again. Why could he never get the radio in the center like in a sandwich, or in the beginning like a sentry, stopping him from walking further into his listening? Why always on the end, ending his thinking of their talking? No, not the end. The big boiled blue intestine eyes and buck teeth yelling: "Hey, shut that off, will ye? Shut that off, Toots. What the hell do we need with a radio anyway?"

When that was ended with a silence, the old man sat back, laughed, tittered and laughed again, very far inside of him, all over him, so that he glowed and his back hurt, then snapping the mouth shut like an old purse, too loose to make a click, afraid they'd hear his cackle-laugh and Toots, with reddish pig-tails done up for the night, sticking her head around the door and reporting back: "Don't know what the old man's laughing for. He's crazy." Answer: "Well, where's your manners? Don't break in on the old man like that. Never know what he may be doing. Where's all your goddam manners, Toots?"

He tested the bristles on his chin again with the tip of his tongue, and rose to put a soft blue circle around another gray flower, a halo around a saint.

Wish I had a cat. One cat. Needn't be big or noisy, just a small cat. Gray. No, not gray with all that gray wallpaper. Yellow. Satan was yellow when he fell as Lucifer. Lucifers the Dutch called matches. I want a cat, a flame. At least, most old men have cats. No use.

"Never know what he may be doing." He knew what

she meant. No, you never know. Abraham had sons when he was ninety and then some. Those old biblicals had lead in their pencils. Never could tell. Thinking about that was sitting in a big sun, in a burly pasture with bees, basking in your own potentialities, possibilities: if you were so and so and days were biblical and things were different; forgetting the hunger of desire, the yellow cat. Sitting and sunning oneself in warm butterfly thoughts of so long ago. Not the past. "Now, when I was young" (interrupted). But another future, blossoming from his old bones, shoots from the hewn-off trunk of Jesse, the old bundled muscles again pliable, the heart calm like a warm beast in a deep burrow, not like a scared squirrel on an oak limb with dogs underneath.

He walked. He walked and peered closely at each flower he had limned in blue. Peered minutely by the little wall light, false candle, bulb ten watt, faint white lettering announcing it had been stolen from The Marden Institute, fly-specked. Walked softly that they couldn't hear him. Opening the window slowly, noiselessly, it must have taken him ten minutes. Old, the old are patient. The old are like the stars, knowing undisturbed. Hardy said that. The old are like God. Shut in a room with magnificent jungle wallpaper. "Why, doctor, he don't even wanna go outside." The window was open. The earth stood with God's stars on top of it; beneath was the noise. Beneath. Old men never kill themselves. Never, world without end, amen. Did you ever hear of anyone over seventy killing himself? Especially not anyone who has no children. Sometimes, children will make them, you know. Just hang on, tough, can't break, only splinter.

He leaned out; the stars have wisdom and understanding like the aged have. So far out that he couldn't hear the voices behind the door, could just see a dog sniffing along the wall of the next house and a woman undressing. Without caring to watch the woman, or to watch the dog, or to watch the stars; they were all alike. He sobbed, his head getting cold where his hair was thin, where it flagged in something like a breeze. "When the old cry it isn't real tears, honey. It's only because the lachrymal, or what-you-may-call-'em glands are busted. Sure, just like bed-wetting. Oh, no, not yet, but before that comes I hope the Almighty Father takes him away."

The dog was done and gone. The woman also. The stars got blurry. A voice beneath him shouted cautiously, "Hy, Gramp, what do you think you're doing?" He peered toward the shape which had the voice he knew. "Nothing at all, sonny. Isn't it time for you to be in bed?" Also cautious, the old and the young conspiring against the stagnation of the ages in between. Peering harder, against the stinging at his eyelids when the voice came upward again. "Sure enough, Gramp. How about you?" The dog once more, snuffling toward the boy shape. "Yes, I think I'll turn in. Tomorrow's another day. Good night, boy."

Pulling his head in, a turtle encasing himself in his misery. Tomorrow another day. Must make oneself fit to cope with another day. The turn always comes tomorrow. Just one fraction of a second may bring it. The unexpected, its grandeur, the end of the long bead-string of hopes. Old men only pass away. They don't do anything themselves to help it along. That wouldn't be venerable.

They would never be honored as they are. On tomorrow's radio, a birthday party for all the dear old ones—we are so proud of them! "Christ, Toots, don't bite your nails like that." Tomorrow is the honey to which the bees fly.

JEAN GARRIGUE

the snowfall

SHE WAS very good-looking: anyone would have to admit that. But her good looks had come to her as a surprise for even through high school she had been thin and sharp-faced. The chagrin of her looks had so impressed her then that she had really never had time to adjust to the new face in her mirror. She still really saw a girl with big cat eyes and a cat-thin face, straw-colored hair lying in wispy uncertainties over the top of her head where sharp ears should have stayed. Her good looks had, in fact, come late: not really appeared until she was twenty-one or so. Suddenly then the hungry boniness of her had disappeared: her shoulders seemed less narrow and hunched, there were amazing tendernesses of contour at the waist, her hair had deepened in color and she had let it grow long.

She had gone through high school and college indifferent and cold, scornful of the tomfool, meaty boys so interested in games and machinery. At twenty she was still actually a child: her social vanities needed no reassurance for she was trying to be a good painter and succeeding—her teachers praised her. But then she had grown up into beauty. It made a great change in her life. She met Tom, who was determined to take her over and scout the nonsense out of her head. They spent an out-of-door summer together. She was good with a gun and had no squeamishness about breaking one syllable of a sparrow's note in two, bursting it midway in air. She was even better than Tom and he had gone to military school and worn royal blue capes! This prowess which—it is true—she bragged of, irritated him and he had set out to break her will in other ways: he realized that she was aloof, physically, not caring to be touched. So he was determined to get her that way, and he did. He was absolutely ruthless and remorseless, he did not care if he nearly broke her arms and when she would bite him because there was nothing else she could do, he was filled with such a pleasant rage that he nearly loved her more than ever.

She herself was painfully and bitterly confused, for she was able to mock him intellectually, to deplore his tastes and ambitions, and yet to welcome the savagery that exerted itself between them. Not that she ever admitted that she liked his callous way of saying: "Yes, you will," but the tension was harshly alive and exciting. Couldn't she admit that? It was exciting. She liked, suddenly, the contours of his mouth: heavy and wide, his hair falling flat over his eyes, the strange fur on his shoulders and back that made her feel as if she were touching a beast.

But the struggle exhausted her—this pure blank hatred she felt for him because he managed to be stronger than she and could pin her down like any sickly insect—and yet, on the other hand, this desire to struggle with him that her hatred might be inflamed so that later it could be subdued. Well, wasn't that it?

It worried her, as well, that there was no sweetness attached to her feelings: no kind of joy. He tormented her, taunted her, bullied her; he never spoke of her painting and she never permitted him to see anything she had done, as if that would be a last sacrilege. It was not until after she had known him for a year that it occurred to her that there was really a kind of immorality at hand, that she was bossed by him not because *she* loved him or even desired him, but because some black motion in her drove her toward him. Once she realized this, she considered it as an abasement and then at last was able to break it off. But the need for reassurance by the male had become a hunger she could not do without, and she had a series of affairs: getting great gifts, records and fountain pens and books.

This energy of interest served to extrovert her. She had not become proud of her looks but interested in them as if they were some distant favor conceded to her, like a newly discovered and romantic relation. Yet profoundly at heart she remained celibate and distrustful, distrustful not of those boys she knew who were incapable, in fact, of tricking or shocking her, for she had made certain, after Tom, to pick those more tractable; but distrustful of the good of the feelings they aroused in her.

She was wary, alert, high-strung, in short, a light sleeper, subject to sudden disorders, and picked at her food. On parting with Tom she had developed an illness that puzzled two doctors. They hesitated, actually, to call it only "nerves" and had put her to bed for a month. During that time she had wept regularly, had been unable to sleep or eat, had lain back against herself, a light shadow on the substantial bed, her lids protecting her eyes. "What is it, what is it, can't you tell me, if only you would tell me!" her father implored. He had taught her to beat him at tennis and to shoot better than Tom. He took a presumptuous, passionate interest in her.

But she had not known herself: shaking her head slowly, as the tears seeped vulgarly out, the color of lilac or shadow, she had not been able to say.

She had met Nicholas in Chicago where she was teaching in a private school and at first she had believed that she might very possibly be able to love him. For he was an artist: she no longer had the problem of trying to make herself understood: he knew what subtleties might awake that gratitude so infrequent in her, and counted on the small: the flower or a print, the right silence, to accost her with the appreciation that was the nearest to love she had come. He was not always yearning at her feet. He was intelligent and immensely talented: a violinist, he played in the Symphony. This was the first man worthy of her, she might admit to herself! She had scorned and ridiculed those others until they had learned to ridicule themselves.

How near she was to love for Nicholas! But what was it—at some mysterious last point the reservation had to be made, the dread qualification. "I love you, however . . ." However, it was true that he was plain and underfed. However, it was true that she admitted once to a friend that she could not quite see taking him into a nightclub. But you never go to nightclubs, her friend answered, and that was true, she never did. She should be ashamed for making so feeble an excuse! Then what was it? What was it that stopped in her, on the threshold of declaration? She had no virginal reluctances, no qualms about committing herself to the long escapade of a love affair, bout after bout, sorty and sally and volley of wills. What was it that balked like the mule at that suggestion of the permanent? She could not say, except that it was the instant that had always moved her, never the funereal threat of continuity. It was the necessity of the endowed instant. As if music were suddenly remembered inside her when the right time for wooing occurred, when she, that is, willed it. She realized that the immense virtue of Nicholas lay in just his sensitivity to her: he actually waited for her first stalking move. His love was so strong and fearful that he dared not risk forcing what he valued upon her. She had to be willing and ready: he had to be sure of the fact. She had become, in her own nervous and resonant way, her own clanging, brisk and jaunty, cocksure fashion, the male and he the compliant, watchful, studious female. He reflected, then, her directions, and it was his task and cleverness to do so. This she immensely admired, and for the first time in her relations with any man felt strong and free. Luckily, too, he tempered his praise of her with occasional outbursts of chill and spare invective. She was not the bitch and louse of criticism's usual hurt spendthrifty. Those criticisms were but another way of expending admiration! and demanded but laughter or the return of insult: bloody, murderous hacking: "You've got nothing in your head." "You're cold and dull." "You fool, you."

But his was reflective, bony comment. She feared his insights because they came from profundities in him that shamed her. She wished she could see him so clearly. It made her feel jealous and slightly inferior. At the same time, it was a consolation (despite her resentment of it) to know that he so had her "interests at heart." She really felt that he knew her better than she knew herself with whom she lived so irregularly. She asked him advice as she might have asked her father had he glossed her with as much clarity of love.

Yet she had taken the job at Yellow Springs, had precipitantly, in the month of September, left Nicholas to be alone in a small town to teach young girls the amenities of water colors.

In her heart she was fearful of going. Once she had made the decision she seriously wondered why she did not stay in Chicago and marry Nicholas. She did not really want to be alone. She felt that she should be but she did not want to be. She was forcing herself into a difficulty. And yet the decision was not a calculated one. A restlessness had made the decision. It awoke her at night and turned her from Nicholas. It criticized and belittled. It made Nicholas a foreign, slavish little dog. It detached her from him, making her cool to his enthusiasms. It made her think: no, this isn't my life yet. Besides, his parents hate me (which was true) and my parents think he is a lame duck (which was also true). It forced all kinds of ridiculous, out of the way and untrue judgments upon her. But in the end it remained that she had to get away.

She was even prepared to hate Yellow Springs. But that inland, sweetened country took her by surprise. It was morning-like and new. She felt that for a long while she could be content with her new, abstemious life: living in a girlish room in somebody's house, teaching classes and holding conferences, painting and saving her money so that soon she could take a year off and study seriously in New York. (Nicholas would come too.)

For as she had grown up belatedly and with a certain amount of aversion to the process, so she had timidly approached her talent, one hand held in back of her? Time? She had an infinite amount of it and as for those powers in herself—well, she firmly and uncritically believed that life would see to it that she deepened and darkened. So, at the age of twenty-three, she was not yet ready for the responsibilities of her desires and possibly Nicholas' eager willingness to assume responsibility for her, to wrap her around with his verities and hopes and to support her intellectually by all the thinking he had done on history, poetry and philosophy, had driven her from him. Possibly she had feared that she might not grow up with him. Possibly she feared that his love stood between her and the blows actuality had not yet given her. For she did fear the laziness in her, that might prevent her from feeling all that she should feel. Oh, she had fine ways of protecting herself from the full consequences of situations! A healthy convenience for black-outs! How well the obdurate memory failed when the ego could profit therefrom!

Well, looking back upon it now, walking through the bitter-bright rindy leaves of first windfall, she could not really understand why she had left Nicholas. He had been the first not to force reproaches upon her, not to make her feel that she was lacking in primal femininities. Looking back over the laundry list, the library catalog of boys she had known, since that unlucky initiation with Tom, she realized that she had permitted all of them to make love to her so that afterwards she would be unable to forgive them for it. But with Nicholas that action had not seemed a disguise for the attainment of blunt supremacy. But especially! she had not felt humiliated by being exposed to her own coldness. At last she did not feel that she was being the dupe of others' desires, the ready jewel-eyed player queen, a stake for others but heartless to herself. So she could then "afford" to be kind to him, could then relax for the first time, since she trusted him. The competitiveness and hostility, the sardonic allegations could be given back to their falsities. He loved what he saw and did not see. Indeed, how interesting to herself his love made her!

But yet—she had had to be free. His love still kept her away from the world. It was still the petition to her vanity, it was so pure and warm, so devoted and sorrowful—a kind of less complicated father-love.

Yes, she had bolted like a thief. Why did Nicholas allow her to go so easily? Possibly because he had reasoned: she is going to a small college town, to teach in a girls' school where they specialize in horseback riding and by the end of the year, after having met only young faculty darlings who sway as they walk, and young well-wived husbands and old salt and pepper deans, and having seen America's sons of the filling station and fire department, ruddy, agog young men born on another planet, she may know that, after all, it is I she has been searching for all her life and I who have accounted for all her unusual lonelinesses in the middle of her fashionable popularities.

And, parting with her, he casually turned over to her his battered but racy and strong Ford coupé. I would simply be paying garage rent here, you know, he said. Now that you won't be here to take rides I'll practice instead. What about other girls, Nicholas? she asked. They can walk, he said.

He wrote her daily, long journal-like letters. Sometimes he felt that he was the curator of a remarkable bird, the last of its species! Would not this account for his watchfulness? But the bird in order to live must go away, must understand more of the world before it could thrive in the great cage of air where he had willed that it must "settle." It must not be hungry for freedoms whose emptinesses it had never tested.

Yes, watchful Nicholas was also cunning, with the foresight and insight of great desire. It was as if his humility and generosity were not character traits but mere extracts and, at the same time, mere placations of the necessity she had become to him. Her ignorant wilfulness, her errancies—merely the excess of her charm! The headstrong moodiness with which she protected her sensitivities—it had frightened all away from that which she truly was. Let him be the Pygmalion to startle her soul!

And she, walking on streets of little houses where pear leaves, dark brown and red, like pyres of light were heaped, was happy and at peace. His letters like literature came, budding with comparisons of her to the dark summer. It was wonderful to be away from him and to have only his letters, his thoughts and her memories. Could she not see him now in his true magnificence? She need never look up to find his eyes, full-lidded, mournful and black in the boniness of his face fixed on her with an expression that was—really—spaniel-like. The way he dressed need not disparage him now—those shirts with flabby collars, the trousers that were always too long and the coat that made his shoulders narrow. Some people could not learn to dress. Nicholas was one. It was the same with his room. Cigarette ashes and dust. Unwashed milk bottles. Discarded razor blades. Month-old newspapers. Torn window blinds. And yet he lavished such care on a phrase, he would work hours to perfect a trill. There was no correlation, she knew, as he had told her. Nevertheless, it disturbed her, and always his slight smell of violinist's nervous sweat, the way he could get his fingers ashy putting out a cigarette! But now, in the absence of those irritations perhaps she could begin to see him with the joy of the soul's eye, she thought, having been educated by him to this.

And indeed she did. She even considered seriously for the first time fidelity. More than that, his ever-recurring appearance by letter fed and sustained her, an aerial diet delicately intoxicating! She went from letters to classes, zestful and proud, and, walking on the old Victorian campus, thought for the first time: I can really dispense with all but the world! Watching the bees stupefied by the rank sweetness of pears gone soft and brown, and grapes in arbors split open by the warmth of the sun, she was tenderly content as if the Autumn promised improbable happiness she did not have to run to.

She went to her first party in Yellow Springs with a red-haired Professor of Radio, a spotty, conceited character lording it over with his voice as if every individual were a crowd. On meeting her he had decided immediately that she was to be his girl for the year. And she, observing distantly the standard ways he took to indicate his liveliness, thought: how is it that once I took pride in leading a fool by the nose?

At the party she was introduced to Luke Banford who sat on a thin chair in a corner, idly fiddling with a pad of paper on which, as she noticed quickly, he had drawn a few caricatures. On seeing him in a gray checked suit which fitted so aptly his moderate tallness and flatness, on seeing his hair, black as a seal's wet fur, his high, polished dark forehead, his eyes, aloof and steely as a bird's with a glance that cut because of its brilliance, his full, wide mouth, so amply balanced and darkly molded, she felt a sudden anger of distaste. Male beauty, made by a watchmaker!

The party bored her and she soon acquired a headache. Do let us go, she said to the Professor who had been cracking jokes with Banford which she had not bothered to listen to. I suggest we all take a ride, the Professor said munificently. What about Starr Lake? It's the last night of Indian Summer they say. She looked up warily to intercept Banford's black glance like ice. Why not? he said, looking at her without smiling. She noticed then a deep, blunt scar on his forehead.

But she said: "Why not?" and turned away. The dark man flushed and the Professor frowned. A moment later he drew her away into the center of the room and said: "Hey, take it easy. He's really a nice guy. I knew him in New York."

"Then what's he doing in Yellow Springs?" she asked.

"He was in a crack-up last year. His wife was killed."

"A sad story," she said.

Riding in the Professor's roadster, a hostage between the two men, the Professor leaning warmly toward her, Banford drawn tautly into a corner, she suddenly felt enormously energetic and cruel. As her father had squeezed through the barbarities and inanities of domestic depressions and business failures by kidding Existence, so she at such times took it out on the world with a brazen, vaudeville wit. Usually her excitement came from ambivalences of tensions, deploying between the erotic and sudden confusing memories that enraged her. She felt herself to be on a ferris wheel then, circling, lifting and dropping over areas of the unknowable. Frightened, she laughed it off, reforming and socializing the nightmare. At such times she wished to turn on herself and kill or mutilate and so chose the world as a worthier object. Nicholas had hated her in such moods but Tom had always laughed with her. Now she noticed that the Professor did too, though he was awkwardly interrupting to lean across her to say to Banford: "She's really got a heart like ducksoup. She's the kind to want to stop a car if she hears some animal crying in the woods."

But even to this Banford, for all his wealthy politeness, scarcely responded and the Professor laughed alone but perhaps more out of relief than enjoyment, for usually he was a part of the world her surgical humor gashed.

But as they stood out in the wind by the lake her joke-book mood dropped away. She was aware of the handsome man's silence and remembered what Nicholas had said of those parties of malice: "It is a way of defaming the world." The wind roughly blew at her and she wished to run straight to the cold mouth of the water.

Sometimes she would meet Luke Banford on the campus. He walked Indian straight, stepping as lightly, with narrow feet, usually his wrist-watch hand in his pocket. He never wore a hat but the wind did not seem to touch him; his hair was always of a piece with his head, black and shining like mica, and his eyes so critical, so glittering beneath the evenness of his proud eyebrows. Occasionally he walked with her, but they never seemed to manage to say much—talking with him was like talking against a waterfall, difficult, as against frightful pressures he built up against her: of silence, of formality, the niceties of caution. She was ready to give it up, simply to pass him by briefly when they met. Besides, she thought, he must really be stupid. And she decided that he had no character.

Then she thought the more of Nicholas, hurrying to his image as if it were an icon in a corner. What an ample and noble life he lived! Always at the heart of sound! But she began to harry his image; she began to drive and hurry it. Less frequently would it appear between unexpected interstices of time, the rough dark head. And sometimes at night, thinking of him, she could find no flavor of joy at all. The image could then assume no life nor body of its own, could neither rustle with sound nor burn with light. My heart must be empty, she thought fiercely, putting her hand against it. And her mouth felt dry.

Suddenly the year began to hurry to its death. A cold wind one morning cut all the leaves down. Rain followed, to soil them. Midway from classes that afternoon she met Luke.

The melancholy of the day had quieted and humbled her. She shivered in the wind as she stood talking to him. He said: "Will you have a drink?" and took her by the arm. The warmth of his hard, delicate hand pierced through her coat and dress sleeves. The abrasive effect of his misfortune had, up till then, made him seem cold and self-insulated—as if by vanity, she had even thought! But now, walking in the sodden afternoon, he seemed less brittle, incalculably more free and direct with her. Perhaps the sadness of the rain!

And sitting with him in the dark light of a tavern she evasively looked from his scar to his mouth and then to his crisp collar. She noticed his fingers, pointed for a man, and the few small hairs on the back of his hand. Suddenly the sight of his scar pained her. The imperfection on perfection. And it seemed that from that short, blunt mark his pain must flow. For surely his silences covered over a dark space of what—some suffering no one could get to! And it seemed remarkable to her that so handsome a man should be so dark and unreachable—so alone, for instance, at the party!

The subtle and petty resentments she had held against him—those neat marriages of color in ties and socks, the hardness of his head and eye, the rebuke of his distant and impersonal indifference, were then revoked. Looking at his scar, she began to marvel as if he had been accused of some grotesquerie. Certainly it then distinguished him. Pity, pity! This is what she exclaimed later. I learned to pity him!

As he was lighting her cigarette, his hand touched hers, and the effect, as though he might have held the flame to her fingers, made her heart freeze with subtle fear and anticipation. They talked in many directions eagerly but carefully, until he said: "I had been planning to leave this town until I met you."

She trembled but sipped her martini as if she were concealing a tear. When finally she looked up at him his eyes were still on hers: black and tense as an animal's. She could not see beyond their surfaces of light. The black kept out the color of his thoughts.

From then on she saw him constantly, for dinner, for long walks, for drives in Nicholas' Ford to the show parts of the state. Those with whom she had been about to make friends she forgot had ever interested her. She went from classes to him. His looks made him seem remarkable, like some foreign trophy of war and honor. She felt that he wore armor, delicate, invisible, and his aloneness gave her a superstitious belief in his integrity. This exhilarated her because she felt that he had been wounded.

He did not mention what had–as she understood from the Professor–changed his life. He had only told her that he had moved around for the last year, had been up and down the West Coast, in Wyoming, St. Louis, all kinds of places he had never seen before. But it was those very allusions, intensities of gaps between the unfinished accounts of years, that touched her. What time she did not spend with him she spent in her mind with him, finishing out his history, supplying connectives between small anecdotes he related about Hartford, Connecticut, where he had grown up and the year he'd gambled in Wall Street and lost his shirt. But he treated his past gingerly as if it were unfriendly to him and so she too politely pretended to herself that she did not wish to know about it. Yet she conventionally wished him to move in her head sequentially when actually he seemed to have been born from the scar on his forehead. His Spanish eyes and English nose. His sad, cool blood and hawk-like heart.

In a month she was completely in love with him. It did not shock her when he asked her to marry him. She had been so taken by surprise that it seemed inevitable that at last she had pulled out of her sleeve the ace of hearts. In fact, for the first time in her life she did not think about herself. Luke's image completely objectified her. It concentrated her as well. All thought and emotion ran from her to him. She could have been fanatically happy. For at last she was directed, caught up in a single purity of attention and desire. But yet she would be threatened by tears as, sitting by Starr Lake on Saturday afternoons, geese flew over. Uncontrollable, unreasonable sadness! Was it because he was restless with his measly job and talked of Wall Street deals, thereby frightening her? She could only see money gained as money earned.

She wished to put her sadness to some practical cause. For her heart beat so fast, with such elation! And his delicate Indian tread, the steel in the center of his breast so compelled her to moody symbols. She dreamed of ways in which to paint him: with red silk scarves, a blasphemy of softness, tied round his throat.

In that month her looks changed. She grew rosy, and moved so tenderly that everyone remarked: She's a changed person—for one thing, always so gay! She put up her hair, which added a city dignity to her pointed, child-like face. But it was not that! A look in the eyes! The points of her pupils had been absorbed, as if she were always looking into the sun, and all the green of the iris suffused her glance.

Yes, for a month she had no time to think about herself and indeed continued to write to Nicholas as if nothing had happened to her or as if, rather, Luke had given her a new self which had nothing to do with the selves Nicholas had known. Then, in middle November, when he wrote her that he was coming down to see her, she awoke with a start and wired him that it was impossible for her to see him. After that she tried on several occasions to write him the letter that would cut him off from her but each letter was too blunt and exultant. She did not want to boast about her new-found happiness for then it seemed unreal. Actually, she did not want to talk about it at all. It was too private a revelation. When Nicholas finally called her long distance she was rude and stormy. He who had believed he could best keep her by leaving her alone when she made it clear that she wanted to be left alone, broke out into great anger and vowed that he was coming straight down to see what had happened to her. Freed by his rage, she was finally able to write him the letter that told him it was all over and that she was to be married soon. With that gesture she turned her back on all her past and made Luke the king of her eye.

Yet, had she not been able to pity him, who knows what would have happened? Pity was the solvent. The glamor of the automobile wreck! His wife killed by that! He, exempt, but not from remorse and pain, cast out like any wanderer by the guilt he felt. Yes! Pity for this aloof, metallic, glittering man who seemed, physically, as incorruptible as a statue, lent impulsiveness to caution. He was elusive. He was mysterious. He was not knowable because his very appearance so satisfied the eye that the eye wished to stop there, content with the secrecy and reserve that the beautiful must have for protection. As the thorn must safeguard and give dignity to its rose!

Commonplaces, homelinesses, like their cow-licks and ingenuously large ears, had been all the deeps of those she had known before she met Nicholas. Goodnesses and practicalities and shrewdnesses. That kind of single-hearted devotion, intent, possessive but also detached, she had known in Nicholas. But in Luke, there was the great feeling of the pit, that steep fall, that downward rush into perils and dangers, the gambled card, the risked life, the conquering contempt, the disdain, the destruction.

In a few weeks they were always together: she deserted her studio save for those occasions when he would come there to let her sketch him. He was in a dream, a masked dream, filled with loathing of what he had come to, teaching a class in radio in Yellow Springs after years of sailboating off Long Island and commanding stone houses on the seacoast. But the sickness still so hidden by his hard breast she would cure, she believed. That sense of responsibility for so obscure a charge exalted her. And he was good to her in a purely self-absorbed and penitent way; he permitted himself to be taken care of by her. When suddenly he had to go to New York on business he accepted the loan of Nicholas' car and even some money she jokingly gave him although he had flushed and had said crisply: "My poor foolish proper girl."

The week that he was gone she hated the canvas color of the sky and the bare, ruined trees and could think only of the fanciful, proportioned life he would, with casual elegance, ordain for her. And when he returned, having wrecked Nicholas' car on the way, she was only so glad that he had not been hurt that she could not fret over the embarrassment, to say the least, of the loss.

Of course he did drive ninety miles an hour!

But the car could be repaired. "Think nothing of it," she said. "I don't."

Yet her effort to steel herself against such concern robbed for a while her joy of some of its energy. This did vex for she was immoderately anxious to have everything perfect between them. She was as determined to have him as perfect as he could be and what he had done and had been did seem, in many ways, an intrusion upon the joy his presence brought her. Simply to be in the same room with him! Whereupon she remembered that her mother had said to her: "I just like to be where you are." Ah, well! Then she had turned disdainfully away.

And as when she talked about her own childhood she did not expect him to tell her about his, so she did not expect him to tell her why it had been so necessary for him to go to New York. He had the most subtle ways of keeping such areas of his life fenced off. A silence contracted around him which anguished her but for which she had total respect. He seemed, really, divested of background. She was certain that he had had an easy boyhood but this was simply because he dressed so well and had such fine, easy manners and, moreover, because he had such a talent for letting money go by him, out the window of hopes! This scornful unconsciousness about money worried her for she did feel that he might be the sort of person to get himself into trouble over what he, in his piratical dignity, deemed trifling, the care of bankclerks and prudential knaves.

So she had soon learned to live with a small, cold dread for him, unnamable, based upon nothing but fluctuations of intuition. Those fears accounted for sudden tendernesses toward him that were her own miracle. She had never before been so human, so "womanly." But those others had presented solid, impermeable surfaces; the face-hardened opinion, the dogged conviction. She in her uncertainties had had to proceed against such certitudes, her footing untenable on such resistant, tensile bluffs. But he was dark shade, the cool and fear of subtile caves. His silences were stony and hawk-like but softness also spread out from them. There were things he did not want to say. There were strengths he wished to preserve from glaring speech. He did not have to be anything with her but a breathing thing: a dark object of blood and black hair and bird-black, icy eyes.

Yet he saw that, at occasional parties, she did not drink too much and studied minor landscapes of hers or those sketches she was always making of him with long care and interest. "The sky is too cold here," he would say, or "if you could make this corner more interesting, I should like to hear the *sound* of the bells." "Now the value of El Greco's crooked beards—you make this face too symmetrical." It was his own, a fact both ignored.

Such criticisms seemed gilded. She saw him as the prince of good taste. She admired the disinterestedness with which he listened to scraps of her past: the rebellions at ten, the death of her grandmother, games in which she had won all the marbles from little boys. He was not anxious as Nicholas had been to verify an interpretation of her, painfully anxious to catch more light on the coils of her soul.

She invited him home for Christmas vacation. On Christmas Eve she was so excited, so happy, for snow had begun to fall at twilight and late that night they had gone out for a walk, running into bushes like children and throwing soft, tender bullets of snow at one another, that she said to herself: I fear: this joy brings me too close to sorrow. And at three o'clock that night had gone to his room, once her grandmother's.

"My dear!" he said, "this is incestuous," as he found her weeping beside him.

"Luke!" she begged, "do not leave me."

When Nicholas came down she was immediately outraged to see his dark face like her conscience against the general white.

"I hope you came to get your Ford," she said.

"You can keep the Ford. I wanted to see you."

"There's nothing worse than post-mortems. I said what I had to say in my letter."

"I know you did," he said, "but I didn't believe your truth. But it's true that you've changed. You're all dolled up. Let's see your finger nails."

He seized her hands. She tried to pull them away but he held on to them savagely. There was an intense, invisible motion about him. His rough, black hair looked uncombed. His shirt collar was, as usual, wilted and smudged. He looked into her face as if he held a bright light against it. She avoided his eyes and suddenly he let her hands go with a show of great disgust.

"Yes, I would say," he said methodically, "that there is a change. You have that well-loved look that pretty women around thirty so often get."

"You're insulting," she said.

"But where's the candidate?" he asked. "No pictures around?"

For a moment he paced up and down the room. How undersized and bony he looked! How shabby and hungry! She felt triumphant, thinking of Luke's long, flat and beautiful back, the wide wings of his shoulders. And his delicate, narrow ankles!

Suddenly Nicholas stood before her. "Why have you done this?"

"I am in love."

"But you have made a mistake," he said studiously. "There is only one for me and that is you and there is only one for you and that is me."

Her heart hardened. "I could never love you," she said.

"What does he want to give you? A house in Indian Hills?"

"Keep him out of it," she said fiercely.

"How could you have changed," he asked thoughtfully. "I believed you wanted to be a painter. It seems you want to be a wife. Just a beautiful doll of a wife. Just a loving, fatuous spouse."

"Get out," she cried, pained and hurt.

"Now I have made you angry. But what have you done to me? You are going to make me suffer. I don't like that. Can you understand how I wish to protect myself and how I would do anything, anything, to make you realize that I am the one for you?"

"I have found the man I love," she said stonily.

"Was it such deception?" he asked, grimacing.

"Did I ever tell you I loved you?"

"But you might as well have. We might as well have been married. No one could have known you better than I! You allowed me to know you. All your miseries, ambitions and memories. If you can forget, do you think I can?"

"It was all a mistake."

He paled. "Then you are killing our two years. Two years is a great deal of space and time to kill. I don't think you will succeed."

"How dramatic you are."

He went on as if he did not hear her: "In the winter there is only One. Is it because the streets are so cold? The world shrivels up like an old orange. Passion becomes so inward, it is in all the pores and secret veins. It *is* the body. In the spring it is different when the world expands and goes outward. The wits of the heart get crafty then.

Do you want me to forget you? Is that what you want?"

She looked at him hurriedly and then turned away. In her heart she could not find it possible to say yes! forget me! The way in which he knew her was a consolation! Even his ridiculous manner of treating her as a museum piece. Stay! Just that way! he had commanded her, just so against the light!

She looked out to the snow. Did she want him to forget her? He had discovered so much of herself for her.

He came up to her. She saw a heavy sorrow standing in his eyes. He took her by the shoulders. But the instant that his nervous touch was upon her she was glad. Oh, I cannot really love him, she knew. False sympathy! Sentimentality! He's nothing to me! He was never my soul. It's that he talked so well. His rhetoric bewitched me.

Please go! she said, and moved away from beneath his hands.

He said no more but looked at her. For a moment yet the reasonableness of his pain struggled with her. But suddenly realizing that what she wanted to do she did have the courage to do—but yet not want to do and cringed to do when he did not touch her but only looked at her—she said:

"Here are the keys to the Ford."

She threw them at his lank chest, and walked out of the room, leaving him there.

This then, more than anything, gave her completely and wholly over to Luke. She need not be obliged to remember Nicholas' nose when she admired Luke's; to think how both men were so dark, but Luke so golden dark and

Nicholas so blackly dark, like a coal-miner; she need not remember that sometimes—such was the sad universality of language!—Luke said the phrase that Nicholas had once said.

But there was a difference! She felt obliged to consider the relation anew, from a distance. Nicholas' leavetaking had robbed her of some very imperceptible but dense and alive background. Now no one stood in the mirror but Luke and herself. That older, obscure penumbra of image, the subtle prod to her conscience, now gone, left her all the more dramatically alone when Luke was away. Now she was feverish, her body felt alone and abandoned. For two months the sun did not shine and Luke had resigned his job at Yellow Springs and had taken a job with the new radio station in her home town. It paid him better and he needed money, he jocularly confessed. He had debts in New York that might catch up with him.

But then he had turned around and bought a brisk and handsome second-hand roadster for them, as he put it. Every weekend he drove its wheels off to see her; two hundred miles each way. She knew how fast he drove and how destructive his impatience could be. But yet! the winter was so black and arid! What would she do without him? She had made no friends in Yellow Springs. She was absolutely dependent on him. The Professor, sternly disapproving of the choice she had made, avoided her. Two casual acquaintances—serious but charming young women—had said to her on separate occasions: "But he seems so superficial!" She had darkly thought that they had conspired together to present the same judgment to her, and had been bitterly offended as she had violently distrusted her father after he had said one night when Luke had gone out for cigarettes: "Are you sure he will make you happy?"

"Am I sure I will make him happy!" she had rejoined.

"No, my dear," he had begun with his best Polonius air, "a man does not depend on a woman for happiness. What a man wants is the difficult. He wants to fight. He wants to buck up against stone. He wants to feel his courage and muscle. Now Luke: are you sure he wants that? Are you sure he isn't looking for the perpetual golf course?"

"Oh, she could have turned upon him! She could have said: You old cotton-mouthed fool! You kill-joy you! But she had not. Her father, for all his insulting sententiousness, loved her piously and wanted to see her well married to a home, wanted for her all the safeties he had sought so feverishly, and all the dullnesses. But that he had dared to speak of Luke! No one dared use his name but as she allowed them to. Oh! to answer him, to say: You don't even know whom you're speaking of, please dismiss the subject, I will not have the ignorant speaking of what I love—it was rude, too shocking. It would rankle in her conscience afterward. Thank God, at that minute Luke had come back, the brim of his hat holding snow like daisies. "Darling!" he had exclaimed. And that word, falling so clemently, with the effect of propitiation, between them, a word he rarely confessed to before her parents, exposed the full humiliation of the injustice done him. She had gone up to him, kissing him straight on the mouth, and had stood there, against the tight glances of the two. Luke had stiffened beneath her kiss, which had increased her anger that he should have had to feel its apology.

So she was alone and every Friday night he raced like a speed-king to her. She was alone but yet she could have begged him not to come. For every late Friday night she felt gripped by some agony as if the car were driving through her brain. Occasionally she dared say: "I hope you want to live long, Luke."

"I'm careful," he would state. "I'm an expert."

And then she would be blankly silent.

Yet what would she do, she asked herself, if he did not come every week? For she was quite alone. Nicholas had been right. In the winter there was only One. The world contracted to One. And she waited each Friday for his arrival so that she might come alive.

At first Luke had said: "Let's marry at Christmas." But then she agreed with him later on that it would be better to wait until the summer.

"Why not a house in Indian Hills for a while?" he suggested.

"Oh, Luke," she had replied, abashed. "What do you want from life?"

"You," he had answered conventionally. "I'm spoiled. You're really all I want."

But looking up with the instant delight that statement had borne, she was oppressed by the look in his eye which had not become more brilliant from the influence of those gold words, and as he drew her to him was disappointed by the regular clop of his heart and his beautiful, bitter odor.

And what did he mean, that he was spoiled? she thought anxiously, remembering much later that quality of his voice which seemed to come through from another time, as if the words were too well known to him, through which, it could seem, another voice was speaking? Or was it merely the repetition of that ironic malice he had employed once before when he had said to her as she stood in a doorway in a green dress, putting up her hair: "How strong you are! It doesn't matter if I'm weak, does it?"

It was afterward that she thought: why did he choose February? Of all months dead in the calendar, when hope had been exhausted by the winter, when the long effort against the withering cold had all but mummied the flesh and the heart could do no more than keep up its life against the north, of all times, why had he told her then that it was not his wife who had been killed in the accident but a girl he had been in love with and that it was her death that had nearly knocked him in and that his wife was still in New York.

Oh, Luke! she had said. Oh! the lie! she had thought. The dishonor! she had thought. He had said she must understand: how the story had got started that it had been his wife; the Professor had got it wrong.

"I never wanted to talk about it," he said. "He didn't hear it from me. It was my business. I didn't want the blabbings of others about that. Their questionable condolences: O my God, I've just heard . . . That's why I got away. Everyone saying: tough luck. Her mother. Her sisters."

"You loved her," she said.

He looked up as if she had, in that withdrawn moment, touched him. "Yes."

"Then you met me," she persisted quietly.

He had not heard her. Sweat was on his upper lip.

"It was all useless," he said, "useless."

"Luke, tell me," she said. "I've got to know."

"Oh, the filthy details," he said, striking at the table softly. "Icy road. March.

"She lived in New London. I'd gone up to see her. Sunday night I was going back to New York."

She waited.

"I wasn't going fast. There was a curve. I skidded. Another car was coming. It skidded. We all met. Of course she was with me. I was the only one in the whole bunch to get out alive."

She looked at his scar with horror but then had no more reactions.

A great snow fell. It was thick and strong and broke many branches. It fell steadily on Thursday, stopped on Friday, and began again on Saturday, when Luke was with her in her studio. It made the world look like the inside of a great soft tomb, and what Luke had told her was jailed in it. She felt stunned, but by the snow.

Yet she listened to him as she watched the white grains fall over the sky panes. Were they not falling through? Could the glass stop them? The world was white like the inside of a tomb.

He was saying that he would save money like hell and get a divorce in six months. Idly she thought: he exaggerates. It will take a year. And he will never save the money. He cannot save. He's a prince with money. I can save. I'll buy his divorce.

But she lifted her hand and let it fall, imitating the descent of one particular flake.

"I am not jealous of your wife," she said. "She's a legal dear."

He smiled uneasily.

She looked at him but preferred the snow flakes. They were brilliant. His face had gone inward. In the gray light those individually bright and sharp flakes made, his face was blurred as if a heavy beard covered it over.

"I'm jealous only of what is like myself," she went on. "What was your girl like, Luke? I think she was like myself."

"She was," he said.

"But she's faceless. What was the color of her eyes? Was she tall?

"Luke," she said, starting, "did you like me because I was like her?"

"O God," he said.

She saw that he was bored.

As well he might be! The girl was gone!

She wanted to weep because the girl had died uselessly. Luke had loved her, had he not? He had gone up to see her on weekends. The girl had loved him. She too had feared his recklessness and had driven back with him on that icy night. Simply to save him from excesses of speed. But she had not! And she had not saved him! He had concealed the noble fact of her death for so long!

"If I am like her, Luke," she said, "I'm not real, am I? I'm the second-hand parody of her."

"You're out of your head," he said, smiling, and trying to touch her hair.

She averted her head quickly. "How can you love me if

you loved her?" she cried. "I'm jealous but she's more jealous! The jealousy of the dead is lasting!"

He sought to take her hands. "Anybody loves more than once."

"But there is only One!" she answered. "In the winter there is only One. But in the spring too. In the summer too when swimming is the season and the natural sensuality of the pleasure-seeking will."

He smiled, attempting to draw her close and away from such abstractions.

"No," she said, "she makes you dead too. She loved you and you should suffer and you've not and that makes you dead too."

But he was still smiling, attempting to take her hands.

"Nicholas was right," she said. "Go away, Luke, I am very tired."

"You're sick," he said. "You've got to have a fever."

"I love you," she answered, "but your girl haunts me and I love her more."

Obediently he left. She locked the door of the studio which the school had so kindly given her. The gray, philosophic light of the snow came down.

That girl's the mercury for my looking glass, she thought. Now I know how cold, how practical, how shrewd his heart. I see now how he cares for me, she thought. He cannot care, she thought, as I could not care. Love is the image of ourself until ourself destroys us.

And she wept for the perfect love of the girl and for the perfect love of Nicholas.

MERIDEL LE SUEUR

persephone

WE BOARDED the train at a Kansas town. Its black houses sat low amidst the fields which were hardening and darkening now the summer was over. The corn had been shocked, the seed lay in the granaries, the earth had closed, and now the sun hung naked in the sky. All was over—the festival, the flowering, the harvesting. Dark days had come and I was taking the daughter of Freda away to discover, if I could, the malady which made her suffer.

As the train moved from the station I watched Freda standing on the platform, her round face shadowed by the train as it passed between her and the low sun. The daughter leaned against the window for the last sight of her mother; as we left the town she sat with her small head bent as if half broken from her body.

We sped through the dying country, fleeing through the low land. Upon the fields as they lay upturned and dark, clear to the round swinging sky-line, there fell the eerie wan light of the dying season. The train as it traveled through this dim sea of light became uncanny and frail, touched, too, with the bright delicacy of decay. But upon the daughter of Freda the last light dwelt intimately as she lay half sleeping, like the fields, fatally within the cycle of the dying earth.

Fatigued after the preparations for the journey, she rested in utter weariness. Her black garments hung, about to exhaust her, while out from them like sudden flowers sprang her hands and face. Over her great eyes the lids were lowered and gave to her whole being a magical abstraction, as if she looked eternally within, or down through the earth. Only her mouth had tasted of violent fruit; it drooped in her face and turned red when she coughed, which she did frequently, dipping her head like a blind bird.

As I watched her an old pain brewed within me: a faint nostalgia which had come upon me all my life when looking upon her, or when in the presence of her mother, as if upon seeing these two women a kind of budding came about on all the secret unflowered tendrils of my being, to blossom and break in the spaces of a strange world, far from my eyes and hands.

Just when the round and naked sun hung on the horizon, three bulls, standing in the dim, nether light, turned and loped towards our train.

"The black bull," I said, "looked like your husband's."

She lifted the white lids from her eyes, but did not speak. When I repeated what I said, she turned away without answering and sat with her hands in her lap, her eyes lowered, in an attitude so fatal and hopeless that I knew it was of no use to take her on this train, through these fields, past these rivers and houses to our destination.

Nothing lay in these things that could mitigate her illness. The malady was too deep.

As we sped through the fields, the fantastic conquering of distance threw a magic over us so that terrible and vast things became possible. With the dying of the sun the train traveled through a colossal cave, between the closed earth and the closed sky and I half forgot our departure and our destination.

I have always expected some metamorphosis to take place in Freda and her daughter—a moment when the distant look would, by miracle, go from their eyes and they would reveal their nativity in some awful gesture. Nothing had ever happened beyond the natural ritual of our common farm life. But there came upon me now the old mystic credulity as I watched Freda's daughter sitting motionless, her white lids rounding over her eyes, her face glowing in the gloom.

Lying there, she contained like a white seed the mystery of her origin. The marks of living were slight upon her, for from the first she seemed to carry most strongly the mark of a perpetual death. Paradoxically I thought that because death was her intimate, I could never come nearer her mystery than to her birth on the prairies, in the spring as the first white violets bloomed.

For the women of the Kansas town, shading their eyes, had seen Freda coming from the prairies, walking and carrying the child.

"Whose baby is that?" the women asked her when she had come to them.

And she answered, "Mine." And uncovered for them to see, bending down to them.

"When was it born?" these women to whom birth was a great dread, asked.

She answered smiling, "In the night." And she went into a store and bought some goods with little flowers marked on it in which she wrapped the baby.

That year the days were bright and the earth bountiful. For each ear of corn heretofore, there were now two. The sun ripened all that had been sown. The soil was so hot we could not suffer our bare feet upon it. Freda's lands were the most fertile of all.

Her husband, Frantz, the strongest man in the country, was a plowman. We saw him in the fields, dark and stocky, driving his big flanked horses, astride the black furrows that turned behind him. When he came to our fields we were frightened by his narrow eyes buried in the flesh, and by his hands matted with hair.

Together, Frantz and Freda plowed the fields; there was a feeling abroad that never had Freda sown a seed that had not come to fruition. It was true that for her everything blossomed.

In the spring we met her in the fields or in the thickets, where the first flowers were springing alone. In the full, golden light she came towards us, full-bosomed, with baskets of wild berries hanging on her bright arms. When we ran to her, she gave us gifts, berries, nuts, and wild fruits unknown to us.

At harvest time she worked in the fields with the men. When we brought her water she straightened from the earth to loom above us, curving against the sky; a strong odor would come from her, like the odor of the earth when it is just turned; her yellow hair would glisten round her face and we thought it grew from her head exactly as the wheat grew from the earth. Once when she leaned over me, I grew faint with the fertile odor and at the same time drops of perspiration fell from her temples on my face.

When her mare was seen hitched outside the houses of the town, we knew that a great, natural, and dreadful thing was taking place within. The house became, after that, marked, possessing a strange significance of birth. We children, while the mare waited, sat on the curb watching for Freda, who, when she came, passed in a kind of confusion of her great body, the golden hair, and the strong, sweet odor. We would watch the hips of the horse, with Freda upon her, disappearing down the road, past the houses of the town, out into the open plains.

The child of Freda, delicate and pale from the first, was not much known or seen about. She came to town on the first spring days, with her mother, riding in the wagon, atop the early vegetables. She carried with her always, falling from her hands, the first white violets. It did not astonish us that she was thus privy to the first stirrings of the season, since we glimpsed her through all the year in the prairies, by the streams, or hidden in the nooks of the fragrant hills. In the fall, returning from berry hunting, she brushed past us in the chill dusk. In the winter, as we went to the frozen creek, we glimpsed her peering from the naked bush. In the spring we saw her come by her mother, with the first violets. She never spoke to us, but covered her enormous eyes with her lids, standing quite still, before us but irrevocably hidden.

On Saturdays as Freda went about the town she hid

behind her skirts, her eyes lowered in her slim, pale face. Some women would stop in the streets and say she was idiotic because of her little head. To me, however, she had a strange grace, with her swelling body, her little head and pale face, her eyes like minerals, and her hair light like her mother's, but fine and thin as if it had grown outside the light of the sun.

When Freda and her husband were plowing the fields, the girl, who grew very tall, would run in the wake of the plow, singing. Frantz hated her, as everyone knew, and he hated her singing. When Freda with her horses went plunging through the black waves to the horizon, he would leave his plow and strike at the girl. She would veer away as if only the wind had struck her, still singing.

When I could run away from the town I used to lie in the damp thicket which bordered their field and watch them: the dark man straddling the furrows, following the rumps of his horses, holding the plow to the heavy soil; Freda with her skirts on the earth, the horses turning their great eyes to look back at her, the fields lying about her with their living secrets—I watched with satisfaction these two heavy figures, turning the vast earth, moving upon her stillnesses, and the slim girl, like an antelope, running in the fields beside them, singing high and shrill.

She coughed beside me, dipping her little head like a bird. Now no song was in her.

Outside rapidly past us moved the thickets, the fields, the villages. A woman stood in a doorway, half invisible in the dusk, hoisting a baby on her hip—a man came down the road with his team, the white breath of the horses flying from them in the dusk.

The visible world was sinking into another sea, into a faint dusk. The daughter of Freda lay like a fallen and despoiled angel, traveling through darkness, lost to the realm of her nativity, with neither memory nor anticipation. Still I watched her trying to spin around her the stuff of reality. Did there exist for her the seed of our common life or had she eaten only the fruit of perpetual strangeness and death? All that had happened to her, all the incidents of her life, I brought to bear upon her, but I had easier made a mark upon the wind. These things had made no mark upon her. The only mark was her mark upon life, upon all of us who saw her as a frail lost child in the fields of her mother, as a woman ravished by strangeness.

The young farm boys, still delicate with the wind and the fire which is the mark of light and air before the fields harden them, were the only ones who came close to Freda's daughter. They often told us in the evenings that they had met her in the thickets or coming across the fields, and had talked with her. But then they would say no more.

The older youths found it impossible to snare the footsteps of the delicate girl. Strange to say, on the other hand, the firm and serious farm youth were convinced of her wantonness, while old ladies rocking on their porches hinted dark things of her.

But one night a man came to town, from the West,

driving his cattle, packed and bellowing, through the deserted streets.

The next morning people said to each other, "Did you hear the cattle going by in the night?" We children thought it had been only a dream until, early in the morning, we saw on the lawn the deep prints of cloven hoofs. When I went for the morning milk, just outside the town, I saw the cattle where they stood sleeping, knee-deep in the grass and mist. As I was passing a man sat up, from where he too had been sleeping, and looked at me from the grasses. His beard stood out like bracken. From his low forehead the black hair sprang. When I saw him about to rise, I ran into the town shouting to my brothers that the cattle they had heard and thought were only the sound in a dream, had really gone down our streets, and had stopped on the outskirts of the town.

It came to be known that the man I had seen in the grasses went by the name of March. Saturday he came into the town riding a splendid horse. He went about the streets talking in a loud voice to the country people. He was to be seen too, at the horse barns, or at public auctions. Saturday nights he herded what cattle he had purchased, sometimes only a fine bull, to the pasture he had bought next to Freda's land. He became famous through the countryside for his pedigreed bulls. The farmers came in season to lead them to their own pastures for breeding.

It happened in a very subtle way that the countryside came to think of Freda and her daughter and the man March, all three together, as somehow of the same blood. All the vital acts of farm life came to move around one or the other of them. Freda and her husband seemed intimate with the fields, and the half mystical rites of planting and reaping. It was said in wonder that Freda even brought in the lambs as they were dropped in the fields in the spring as if she knew their time. She appeared to the women at the oven and her appearance augured good bread. It was out their road the farmers went for the breeding of their cows. The very lay of the land with its rich dark color was strange, so was the magic they had with the earth and with natural things. Freda's daughter held a more strange mystery. She seemed half evil at times. But after she saved the life of a boy, when his body had turned black, they sought her out for palliatives.

So that it came about that the country people, as they dreamed over their work in the spring and autumn, were half unconsciously touched by the mystery of their tasks—a mystery between their own action and the secret of what they acted upon, by virtue of which alliance everything they did prospered and yielded in the field, the vine, the flesh. Probably because they were, in a manner of speaking, without a God, when in their dream, in a kind of blind ecstasy over the earth, within the heat, they attributed dimly to the figure of Freda, and with her the other two, an alliance and an intimacy with the virtue and the mystery, along with something sinister, of the natural things of which their lives were made.

After the corn had been husked and the dreary Kansas cold had set in, I was wandering in the thicket which ran along the stream in a little curve of the fields below Freda's. The pale sun, casting no shadow, shone on the naked sod and the land, low and flat, swelled a little to the sky. This side of Freda's the bulls stood in the wind, quite still.

I had just left the path and gone further into the thickets for berries, when, out of the dying woods, with only a slight sound like a bird's, ran the daughter of Freda. March came after her. I could hear his feet strike the bare ground, and saw as he ran past me, his black beard and hair struck by the wind as he ran into the open. She had climbed the barbed wire fence and was running in the bull pasture, through the crisp grasses toward her mother's. But three bulls turned at the farthest fence and eyed her. When she turned back, frightened, March was running to her. Then she stood binding her skirts around her, her small head, like a dying bird's, thrown back. As she seemed about to cry out, he came upon her and bore her with him into the grasses. A young bull struck the ground with his forefeet and loped toward the sun. I ran back into the thicket.

The next days I was filled with terror because of what I had seen. I dared not go upon the road to the fields, or even out under the sky. The third day I came home and there in the dusk was Freda, leaning in our door.

"She is gone," I heard her say.

My mother spoke from the dark kitchen. "And is he gone too, with all the cattle?"

"Yes," said Freda and stood suffering in the dusk. After a while she walked away down the dim road.

Frantz came in the night, knocking and pounding at our door to know where she had gone.

That winter she grew very old. The farmers, through the frosty moonlight, saw her wandering the barren plains.

Children screamed when she approached the town. She seemed like an old woman whose time of fertility has gone. In the nights she came knocking at the doors of the village to ask for her daughter.

That year the spring never came. The flowers died beneath the ground and the fields burned in the sun.

Through the hot days of spring we saw her far off, unreal in the simmering heat. We found her by the old well in our orchard, sitting, sorrowing on the stones, her hair wild and white. We were young girls from school with bright ribbons in our hair. We had come to cool our faces over the black opening of the well and to cry down its sides to hear the sweet, far echo answer us. But when we saw her there we drew together, whispering and peering at her. She rose and came toward us, no longer bright and bold, but still terrible, looming above us. She went among us as we hid our faces in our aprons, stroking our hair and arms, calling each of us by the same name. It was a name I had never heard before and I could never, after that, remember it. She peered at each of us so close that we trembled when her breath came upon us. When she turned her sad eyes to the well again we ran from her in every direction, through the orchard, and for the rest of the afternoon watched her from behind the trees as she sat on the stones of the well, sorrowing.

One evening late in summer, as the land lay still beneath the drought, my brother came from the fields, and standing before us with the heat of the day on his face, he said, "I saw Freda's daughter walking toward her mother's."

That night the country people thought it strange that the first rains fell, plunging ceaselessly into the earth.

The train stopped at a siding amidst the prairies in a sudden silence. The woman, aroused, sat up with her eyes wide open.

"How far are we?" she asked in a light voice.

I answered her very low, "From where?"

Before she could answer a fit of coughing shook her and the train started again.

The lights were lit. She was timid about going into the diner, but at last, with vague gestures, lifting her pale hands she put over her head an old velvet hat and rose and went down the aisle, forlorn and pale, with a kind of assaulted and pathetic dignity.

I came behind her, looking at the tall body as it moved with its peculiar grace. It was like this she had come back to Freda's, with this delicate, hopeless grace, as if she had touched strange fruits and eaten pale and deathless seeds.

After the summer, March had come back, driving his bulls through the street to the old pasture. He had knocked at Freda's door and Freda had given her daughter back to him. She had gone to live in his low hut. When we passed we saw her come out of the door to throw the dishwater over the bare ground. Her thick black skirts, given her now by the women of the town, would be pulling and dragging about her, her little head would swirl up from them, free as a serpent's. After she had thrown the water she would stand still, tall and hopeless, in that terrible abstraction, looking toward us with her blind, deep eyes.

In the diner she seated herself with timid, quick movements, then sat with her eyes lowered. Some arrangement of the heavy skirt annoyed her; she fingered it delicately beneath the table. She coughed, turning her head and frowning. In an effort to suppress the cough the tears started, and did not fall, but hung there magnifying her great eyes. Suddenly, unable to bear the light, she closed them. Again as the lids covered her eyes, by some bewitchment her face became beautiful and eternal. I felt again the imminent metamorphosis as if she were about to change before my eyes and as always in haste as if to prevent a phenomenon which I both hoped for and dreaded, I spoke.

"Did you see the fine bulls that ran toward our train?"

She lifted her eyes and looked at me, but did not answer.

"I believe the black one was the one your husband sold the upstate farmer." She was looking at me. "Did you see the bulls just before dark?"

"No," she said and the answer startled me.

Whether it was the natural desolateness of traveling between places, likely to give to the form of what reality we know a vast and fabulous temper, or the sorrow of the dying year, I do not know, but back in the car, I became desolate and afraid.

For the remaining hours I sat opposite, watching her sleeping. I brooded over her, half expectant as if about to startle from the mist that covered her, the winged bird which was the secret of her being. I watched her with pain as she moved me with her ancient mystery, as of something half remembered.

It seemed to me again that a metamorphosis was about to take place here on this train, going through Kansas, that the bounds of all that I had known would be shattered before me. Lying before me, she lost what semblance of reality she ever had and seemed to glow and live in other elements than I knew.

What strange realms had thrust her forth to be born of her mother in the night, to put upon her the burden of endless movement through fields, upon the earth, through many days under the burden of shadowless nights, marked with the mark of strangeness to be usurped by an unfamiliar man, to walk through unfamiliar places, and to carry unfamiliar burdens.

Watching her glow before me with her terrible veiled identity, a strangeness of everything came upon me and a terror. I felt suddenly that after this journey, in which after all nothing had happened, I should never be the same; that by looking upon her I was partaking of some poisonous drug, like the poison of early spring flowers and the poison of late berries.

I dared not move in my terror, afraid she might stir, but she sat still, preoccupied, with her eyes hidden, dreaming of what she had never forgotten. Cautiously I came near to her mystery. She among us all had known that living was a kind of dying. When in these realms, she had refused to partake of our fruits and so become enamored, but had closed herself in the dream which is real and from which we die when we are born.

Soon now we would come upon the city glittering on the plain, above the bluffs of the river. A terror of all that lived came upon me; a terror of Freda's daughter who lay as if dead, glowing already in the mineral worlds of her strange lord. Because of the terror I said to myself, this woman is only the wife of a Kansas stockman—but who is the stockman? We saw him driving his bulls through the night, but who is he? Who is her mother? We saw her in the ripe fields, and turning the soil to fertility—but who is she?

All in that town came to me, all I had known passed before me, and I said, who are they? And I did not know.

DELMORE SCHWARTZ

in dreams begin responsibilities

I

I THINK it is the year 1909. I feel as if I were in a moving-picture theater, the long arm of light crossing the darkness and spinning, my eyes fixed upon the screen. It is a silent picture, as if an old Biograph one, in which the actors are dressed in ridiculously old-fashioned clothes, and one flash succeeds another with sudden jumps, and the actors, too, seem to jump about, walking too fast. The shots are full of rays and dots, as if it had been raining when the picture was photographed. The light is bad.

It is Sunday afternoon, June 12th, 1909, and my father is walking down the quiet streets of Brooklyn on his way to visit my mother. His clothes are newly pressed, and his tie is too tight in his high collar. He jingles the coins in his pocket, thinking of the witty things he will say. I feel as if I had by now relaxed entirely in the soft darkness of the theater; the organist peals out the obvious approximate emotions on which the audience rocks unknowingly.

I am anonymous. I have forgotten myself: it is always so when one goes to a movie, it is, as they say, a drug.

My father walks from street to street of trees, lawns and houses, once in a while coming to an avenue on which a street-car skates and gnaws, progressing slowly. The motorman, who has a handle-bar mustache, helps a young lady wearing a hat like a feathered bowl onto the car. He leisurely makes change and rings his bell as the passengers mount the car. It is obviously Sunday, for everyone is wearing Sunday clothes and the street-car's noises emphasize the quiet of the holiday (Brooklyn is said to be the city of churches). The shops are closed and their shades drawn but for an occasional stationery store or drugstore with great green balls in the window.

My father has chosen to take this long walk because he likes to walk and think. He thinks about himself in the future and so arrives at the place he is to visit in a mild state of exaltation. He pays no attention to the houses he is passing, in which the Sunday dinner is being eaten, nor to the many trees which line each street, now coming to their full green and the time when they will enclose the whole street in leafy shadow. An occasional carriage passes, the horses' hooves falling like stones in the quiet afternoon, and once in a while an automobile, looking like an enormous upholstered sofa, puffs and passes.

My father thinks of my mother, of how lady-like she is, and of the pride which will be his when he introduces her to his family. They are not yet engaged and he is not yet sure that he loves my mother, so that, once in a while, he becomes panicky about the bond already established. But then he reassures himself by thinking of the big men he admires who are married: William Randolph Hearst and William Howard Taft, who has just become the President of the United States.

My father arrives at my mother's house. He has come too early and so is suddenly embarrassed. My aunt, my mother's younger sister, answers the loud bell with her napkin in her hand, for the family is still at dinner. As my father enters, my grandfather rises from the table and shakes hands with him. My mother has run upstairs to tidy herself. My grandmother asks my father if he has had dinner and tells him that my mother will be down soon. My grandfather opens the conversation by remarking about the mild June weather. My father sits uncomfortably near the table, holding his hat in his hand. My grandmother tells my aunt to take my father's hat. My uncle, twelve years old, runs into the house, his hair tousled. He shouts a greeting to my father, who has often given him nickels, and then runs upstairs, as my grandmother shouts after him. It is evident that the respect in which my father is held in this house is tempered by a good deal of mirth. He is impressive, but also very awkward.

II

Finally my mother comes downstairs and my father, being at the moment engaged in conversation with my grandfather, is made uneasy by her entrance, for he does not know whether to greet my mother or to continue the conversation. He gets up from his chair clumsily and says "Hello" gruffly. My grandfather watches this, examining their congruence, such as it is, with a critical eye, and meanwhile rubbing his bearded cheek roughly, as he always does when he reasons. He is worried; he is afraid that my father will not make a good husband for his oldest daughter. At this point something happens to the film, just as my father says something funny to my mother: I am awakened to myself and my unhappiness just as my interest has become most intense. The audience begins to clap impatiently. Then the trouble is attended to, but the film has been returned to a portion just shown, and once more I see my grandfather rubbing his bearded cheek, pondering my father's character. It is difficult to get back into the picture once more and forget myself, but as my mother giggles at my father's words, the darkness drowns me.

My father and mother depart from the house, my father shaking hands with my grandfather once more, out of some unknown uneasiness. I stir uneasily also, slouched in the hard chair of the theater. Where is the older uncle, my mother's older brother? He is studying in his bedroom upstairs, studying for his final examinations at the College of the City of New York, having been dead of double pneumonia for the last twenty-one years. My mother and father walk down the same quiet streets once more. My mother is holding my father's arm and telling him of the novel she has been reading and my father utters judgments of the characters as the plot is made clear to him. This is a habit which he very much enjoys, for he feels the utmost superiority and confidence when he is approving or condemning the behavior of other people. At times he feels moved to utter a brief "Ugh," whenever the story becomes what he would call sugary. This tribute is the assertion of his manliness. My mother feels satisfied by the interest she has awakened; and she is showing my father how intelligent she is and how interesting.

They reach the avenue, and the street-car leisurely arrives. They are going to Coney Island this afternoon, although my mother really considers such pleasures inferior. She has made up her mind to indulge only in a walk on the boardwalk and a pleasant dinner, avoiding the riotous amusements as being beneath the dignity of so dignified a couple.

My father tells my mother how much money he has made in the week just past, exaggerating an amount which need not have been exaggerated. But my father has always felt that actualities somehow fall short, no matter how fine they are. Suddenly I begin to weep. The determined old lady who sits next to me in the theater is annoyed and looks at me with an angry face, and being intimidated, I stop. I drag out my handkerchief and dry my face, licking the drop which has fallen near my lips. Meanwhile I have missed something, for here are my father and mother alighting from the street-car at the last stop, Coney Island.

III

They walk toward the boardwalk and my mother commands my father to inhale the pungent air from the sea. They both breathe in deeply, both of them laughing as they do so. They have in common a great interest in health, although my father is strong and husky, and my mother is frail. They are both full of theories about what is good to eat and not good to eat, and sometimes have heated discussions about it, the whole matter ending in my father's announcement, made with a scornful bluster, that you have to die sooner or later anyway. On the boardwalk's flagpole, the American flag is pulsing in an intermittent wind from the sea.

My father and mother go to the rail of the boardwalk and look down on the beach where a good many bathers are casually walking about. A few are in the surf. A peanut whistle pierces the air with its pleasant and active whine, and my father goes to buy peanuts. My mother remains at the rail and stares at the ocean. The ocean seems merry to her; it pointedly sparkles and again and again the pony waves are released. She notices the children digging in the wet sand, and the bathing costumes of the girls who are her own age. My father returns with the peanuts. Overhead the sun's lightning strikes and strikes, but neither of them are at all aware of it. The boardwalk is full of people dressed in their Sunday clothes and casually strolling. The tide does not reach as far as the boardwalk, and the strollers would feel no danger if it did. My father and mother lean on the rail of the boardwalk and absently stare at the ocean. The ocean is becoming rough; the waves come in slowly, tugging strength from far back. The moment before they somersault, the moment when they arch their backs so beautifully, showing white veins in the green and black, that moment is intolerable. They finally crack, dashing fiercely upon the sand, actually driving, full force downward, against it, bouncing upward and forward, and at last petering out into a small stream of bubbles which slides up the beach and then is recalled. The sun overhead does not disturb my father and my mother. They gaze idly at the ocean, scarcely interested in its harshness. But I stare at the terrible sun which breaks up sight, and the fatal merciless passionate ocean. I forget my parents. I stare fascinated, and finally, shocked by their indifference, I burst out weeping once more. The old lady next to me pats my shoulder and says: "There, there, young man, all of this is only a movie, only a movie," but I look up once more at the terrifying sun and the terrifying ocean, and being unable to control my tears I get up and go to the men's room, stumbling over the feet of the other people seated in my row.

IV

When I return, feeling as if I had just awakened in the morning sick for lack of sleep, several hours have apparently passed and my parents are riding on the merry-go-round. My father is on a black horse, my mother on a white one, and they seem to be making an eternal circuit for the single purpose of snatching the nickel rings which are attached to an arm of one of the posts. A hand organ is playing; it is inseparable from the ceaseless circling of the merry-go-round.

For a moment it seems that they will never get off the carousel, for it will never stop, and I feel as if I were looking down from the fiftieth story of a building. But at length they do get off; even the hand-organ has ceased for a moment. There is a sudden and sweet stillness, as if the achievement of so much motion. My mother has acquired only two rings, my father, however, ten of them, although it was my mother who really wanted them.

They walk on along the boardwalk as the afternoon descends by imperceptible degrees into the incredible violet of dusk. Everything fades into a relaxed glow, even the ceaseless murmuring from the beach. They look for a place to have dinner. My father suggests the best restaurant on the boardwalk and my mother demurs, according to her principles of economy and housewifeliness.

However they do go to the best place, asking for a table near the window so that they can look out upon the boardwalk and the mobile ocean. My father feels omnipotent as he places a quarter in the waiter's hand in asking for a table. The place is crowded and here too there is music, this time from a kind of string trio. My father orders with a fine confidence.

As their dinner goes on, my father tells of his plans for the future and my mother shows with expressive face how interested she is, and how impressed. My father becomes exultant, lifted up by the waltz that is being played and his own future begins to intoxicate him. My father tells my mother that he is going to expand his business, for there is a great deal of money to be made. He wants to settle down. After all, he is twenty-nine, he has lived by himself since his thirteenth year, he is making more and more money, and he is envious of his friends when he visits them in the security of their homes, surrounded, it seems, by the calm domestic pleasures, and by delightful children, and then as the waltz reaches the moment when the dancers all swing madly, then, then with awful daring, then he asks my mother to marry him, although awkwardly enough and puzzled as to how he had arrived at the question, and she, to make the whole business worse, begins to cry, and my father looks nervously about, not knowing at all what to do now, and my mother says: "It's all I've wanted from the first moment I saw you," sobbing, and he finds all of this very difficult, scarcely to his taste, scarcely as he thought it would be, on his long walks over Brooklyn Bridge in the revery of a fine cigar, and it was then, at that point, that I stood up in the theater and shouted: "Don't do it! It's not too late to change your minds, both of you. Nothing good will come of it, only remorse, hatred, scandal, and two children whose characters are monstrous." The whole audience turned to look at me, annoyed, the usher came hurrying down the aisle flashing his searchlight, and the old lady next to me tugged me down into my seat, saying: "Be quiet. You'll be put out, and you paid thirty-five cents to come in." And so I shut my eyes because I could not bear to see what was happening. I sat there quietly.

V

But after a while I begin to take brief glimpses and at length I watch again with thirsty interest, like a child who tries to maintain his sulk when he is offered the bribe of candy. My parents are now having their picture taken in a photographer's booth along the boardwalk. The place is shadowed in the mauve light which is apparently necessary. The camera is set to the side on its tripod and looks like a Martian man. The photographer is instructing my parents in how to pose. My father has his arm over my mother's shoulder, and both of them smile emphatically. The photographer brings my mother a bouquet of flowers to hold in her hand, but she holds it at the wrong angle. Then the photographer covers himself with the black cloth which drapes the camera and all that one sees of him is one protruding arm and his hand with which he holds tightly to the rubber ball which he squeezes when the picture is taken. But he is not satisfied with their appearance. He feels that somehow there is something wrong in their pose. Again and again he comes out from his hiding place with new directions. Each suggestion merely makes matters worse. My father is becoming impatient. They try a seated pose. The photographer explains that he has his pride, he wants to make beautiful pictures, he is not merely interested in all of this for the money. My father says: "Hurry up, will you? We haven't got all night." But the photographer only scurries about apologetically, issuing new directions. The photographer charms me, and I approve of him with all my heart, for I know exactly how he feels, and as he criticizes each revised pose according to some obscure idea of rightness, I become quite hopeful. But then my father says angrily: "Come on, you've had enough time, we're not going to wait any longer." And the photographer, sighing unhappily, goes back into the black covering, and holds out his hand, saying: "One, two, three, Now!", and the picture is taken, with my father's smile turned to a grimace and my mother's bright and false. It takes a few minutes for the picture to be developed and as my parents sit in the curious light they become depressed.

VI

They have passed a fortune-teller's booth and my mother wishes to go in, but my father does not. They begin to argue about it. My mother becomes stubborn, my father once more impatient. What my father would like to do now is walk off and leave my mother there, but he knows that that would never do. My mother refuses to budge. She is near tears, but she feels an uncontrollable desire to hear what the palm-reader will say. My father consents angrily and they both go into the booth which is, in a way, like the photographer's, since it is draped in black cloth and its light is colored and shadowed. The place is too warm, and my father keeps saying that this is all nonsense, pointing to the crystal ball on the table. The fortune-teller, a short, fat woman garbed in robes supposedly exotic, comes into the room and greets them, speaking with an accent, but suddenly my father feels that the whole thing is intolerable; he tugs at my mother's arm but my mother refuses to budge. And then, in terrible anger, my father lets go of my mother's arm and strides out, leaving my mother stunned. She makes a movement as if to go after him, but the fortune-teller holds her and begs her not to do so, and I in my seat in the darkness am shocked and horrified. I feel as if I were walking a tight-rope one hundred feet over a circus audience and suddenly the rope is showing signs of breaking, and I get up from my seat and begin to shout once more the first words I can think of to communicate my terrible fear, and once more the usher comes hurrying down the aisle flashing his searchlight, and the old lady pleads with me, and the shocked audience has turned to stare at me, and I keep shouting: "What are they doing? Don't they know what they are doing? Why doesn't my mother go after my father and beg him not to be angry? If she does not do that, what will she do? Doesn't my father know what he is doing?" But the usher has seized my arm and is dragging me away, and as he does so, he says: "What are *you* doing? Don't you know you can't do things like this, you can't do whatever you want to do, even if other people aren't about? You will be sorry if you do not do what you should do. You can't carry on like this, it is not right, you will find that out soon enough, everything you do matters too much," and as he said that, dragging me through the lobby of the theater, into the cold light, I woke up into the bleak winter morning of my twenty-first birthday, the window-sill shining with its lip of snow, and the morning already begun.

JEAN STAFFORD

a reunion

LIKE COOLED-OFF lovers meeting again after a long separation, we were excessively courteous. We plied our interrogations with a well-bred inattention to their answers and we diligently observed all those amenities which are calculated to tame a difficult encounter. My father's letter (his calligraphy, I had noted, had neither become less neat nor more mature) had not stated his reason for inviting me to visit him. Moreover, in my reply, I had not told him why I was accepting, and I concluded that we were each activated by no more than curiosity, as the lovers would be, to know what alterations the years had accomplished in the other.

I learned that for seven years my father had, as usual, done a little reading, been occasionally ill, entertained a few guests, and had largely spent his time gardening. He learned that I had had an equal share of bad and good luck. Throughout the first hour of our reunion, coinciding happily (and by no means accidentally) with dinner, we exchanged, like the calling cards of strangers, the names of his guests and the names of the places where I had lived. We pursued the recent tributaries of our lives and never once returned to seek the old meanderings of our mutual experience.

Proud of his garden and because there was a full moon that night, my father took me out after our coffee to show me the gladioli and the dahlias which had commenced to bloom a week or so before. As he stooped amongst them to caress their petals, I noticed for the first time that he was an old man. Livid and sharp as one of his trees in winter, his large and noble nose and his insistent cheekbones had been uncovered nearly to the skeleton, yet, elsewhere, particularly in the hands that quivered as they reached toward the flowers, the skin was too ample an integument and stood up in limp ridges over the bones. He was a small man. Now he seemed even smaller, and he had dried up everywhere save in his brown eyes. He was like one of the bearded weeds that every summer invaded his garden; had I touched his skin, I thought, I would have found it harsh like the hollyhock leaf. Into his voice, which had always been half an octave higher than a man's should be, there had crept the note of senility's sour protestations. Yet, in a sense, he looked exactly as he had when I last saw him: his seven static years had done no more than reinforce what had been there all along.

It was here that I had seen him last. I had told him good-by while he pruned the rhododendrons. Then, I had longed to confirm our kinship by some gesture which, no matter how brief, would unite us for its duration: a look, perceiving me at last from the eyes that benevolently studied the shrub and shears, a clasp of the hands that tenderly ministered to the leaves and blossoms, or a word from the mouth that an hour ago had elegantly and incisively said, "Of course you may stay as long as you like. It is your privilege." I had come out to him, believing that the crisis had not been reached yet, that there was still time to deflect the catastrophe. But he did not look up, and the stretch of grass between us seemed unnavigable. As I stared at him stupidly, a naive tear in either eye, I realized that my misery was gauche for I knew that my father did not see our estrangement in the heroic dimensions that I did. And so I had turned at last and facing the house, my back to him, had said, "Well, good-by." Before he echoed me, I heard, several times, the snip of his shears and the rustling of the rhododendron leaves.

We moved tonight from shrub to shrub and from the bed of zinnias to the rose-bushes, and he murmured that he hoped I was not bored, although he knew I was not interested in flowers ("something, as you remember," he said, "I never understood in you"), but that it was his habit to spend half an hour in the garden every evening after dinner. An abrupt movement in the grass unnerved my citied feet and I asked my father if there were snakes here still.

"Of course," he laughed. "One wouldn't want one's garden to be incomplete. Besides, they kill the spiders."

We slowly approached the far end of the garden where his splendid azaleas were planted and the japonica and where three mountain ash trees dropped their scarlet globules on to my mother's grave. Our advance, deliberate and silent like that of acolytes toward the sanctuary, enclosed us in a parenthesis whose solemnity, for me, was trumped-up, and I, to demolish the ambiguity of my role, said lightly, "How the ash trees have flourished."

"Yes. The soil here welcomes anything. John Stuart, whom you may remember, was surprised when he came to visit me some years ago at my choice of decoration for this part of the garden. 'Red?' says he. 'And something so foreign to us? I'd thought you would plant junipers.' And still, when I had explained my reason to him, he had to agree that I'd been right. You recall the reason? That she loved this special red? I have no doubt other friends of mine have wondered, but they've been too tactful to enquire."

"Too tactful?"

"Why, yes, to be sure. Isn't that a kind of tact? To speak as little as possible of the dead to the bereft?"

He had stopped some paces from the gravestone and had turned away from me to pluck a dying leaf from an azalea plant, but I knew that his face, in spite of the changes of age, wore an expression of anger and yet of satisfaction that I had seen so often from the earliest days of my childhood. For, adroitly, he had trapped me into revealing for the millionth time my ignorance (he had, seven years ago, called it my "willful ignorance") of his grief which, like a precious flower, had under his care become immortal, as fresh, as faultless as on the day she died and I was born. And yet, he liked to coax a canker to its immaculate petals to cherish them the more when he had cleansed them. Just as he was pulling off the limp yellowing leaf from the azalea, gently, so as not to disturb the delicate living tissues of the plant, so he was removing my careless blight from his heart's rose.

He was reluctant to leave the garden and in that hallowed place—for every flower and tree and bush was dedicated like the appointments of an altar—we would not quarrel, not even in lowered voices and not even in the language so shrewdly civil we had used, on the other occasion, to deceive the servants who might be eavesdropping. It occurred to me, seeing him delay our return to the house by examining the soil about the oleanders and rambling thoughtfully about the lily pond, consuming more than half an hour in an aimless survey of his consecrated grove, that if he were able to predict me better, he would like to prolong my stay; for who but I could so often and yet so impotently threaten his exquisite obsession? Whose guilt was so ineradicable? And I wondered if this was why he had written me after so many years: a curiosity to know if I *had* become more predictable, and if he could now check me before I had gone too far. He had been careful to name no term for my visit. At any moment, he might say, as he had done before, "Of course you may stay as long as you like, but surely you are intelligent enough to see that we can never be at peace with one another."

"I have put a new floor in the summerhouse," he said. "Perhaps you would like to see it. If I remember rightly, the summerhouse was all you really cared about in my little garden." He smiled beseechingly at me like the great lady deprecating her "little house" to her poor cousins. Indeed, I had liked the summer house and had often played there, for it was the only place in the garden where I was not haunted by my mother's ghost and by the slumbrous fragrance of my father's offerings to her. One day

I had marked with brilliant blue paint the diamonds patterned on the floor by the sunlight coming through the lattice work. Now my marks, made with an enamel advertised as indelible, were gone.

We sat down on the circular bench, my father gazing out the doorway in the direction of the gravestone, a slab of marble beneath whose ivory surface a clouded rosiness showed through. He spoke almost to himself, "No, of course you wouldn't remember John Stuart." I did not contradict him, though I perfectly recalled his gaunt and sentimental friend who had come, fifteen years before, at the time my mother's skeleton was transferred from the graveyard to the garden. Evening after evening, I heard their low voices behind the closed door of the library. One night, they walked along the terrace below my windows and I heard John Stuart say, "What a saint you are!" And once, when, at my father's request, I had set out before them glasses and a decanter of brandy, he said, "She is the image of her mother." There was a precise moment of silence, and then my father said, "I am thinking of hiring a tutor. Her Latin is very bad." His voice was even and remote with distaste.

"I noticed this evening at dinner," he said, "that your hair seems a little darker." I did not miss the satisfaction in his words. Anything that made me unlike my mother called forth his secret admiration. As always before, I blushed and quickly diverted his attention from my appearance. "Your new floor is handsome," I said.

"Oh, yes," he said, starting. "Yes, it will do very well." As he bent over to look at it, a large black bug scuttled across the floor and stopped near his foot. I saw him shudder and lift his foot to crush it, but he did not. "A spider," he said. "We have a great many of them at this time of year. Some are poisonous." He continued to gaze at it and in a moment slowly lifted his foot again and brought it down lightly, "Not to make a mess," he whispered. I heard a brittle cracking and my father said, "Oh, what a pity. It wasn't a spider, only a harmless beetle."

He had not killed it. The creature struggled with a frenzied energy and worked itself onto its back, then tossed and labored to right itself, waving weary legs, straightening and flexing them, pausing and wildly fluttering them again. It gained a little and lay upon its side, shuttered a mangled wing, and helplessly rolled over on its back.

"It's not dead," I said. "Hadn't you better kill it?"

His smile was mutilated by the moonlight. It was at once inquiring and patronizing. He said, "Why?"

"I don't know. Only perhaps it's suffering."

"Let me allow you to complete the murder," he said, and as I stood up and started to move towards the dying bug, he added, "I couldn't step on it again myself. The shell cracking under my foot gave me a horrible feeling that I was breaking human bones."

"Then I can't *now!*" I cried. I returned to my place. For some time we remained there, watching the beetle's noiseless fit; it seemed hours later that a sudden darkness passed over the floor of the summerhouse and my father sprang to his feet with a cry. But immediately himself again, as though he had not uttered it, as though the sound were as unconnected with us as the distant hoot of an owl, he said, "You must excuse me. I go to bed early, though I don't sleep. Feel free to stay as long as you like. I can send a lantern out to you."

He lighted a lantern he had taken down from the shelf above the bench and his face, illumined briefly, revealed no more than had his voice, the dismay that had made him cry out.

"No, thank you," I said. "The moon will come out again. I can see without it anyhow."

I followed him out the door and lay down upon the grass. I leaned on my elbow and watched him pass through the opening in the hedge. His lantern's arc caricatured him as a ghost out-of-joint; his head was peaked by the phenomenon of the light and in place of arms, two narrow wings listlessly swung while the fattened torso wambled. The sad light diminished and was absorbed. The moon shone forth again and in its light, as I turned and leaned upon the other elbow, I could see the beetle on the floor of the summerhouse still pitching in its morbid dance. I lay back upon the grass and seemed to fall into the depths of the earth with a forcible weariness and closed my eyes and, perhaps for a few minutes, dozed. Then, suddenly confused as one whose dream of last night contradicts or corresponds to today's facts, it occurred to me that the beetle actually was dead and had been from the first and that the changeable moon's ruffling chiaroscuro had misled us. I went into the summerhouse and, stooping down, saw that some time since, its life arrested, death had chosen for its final attitude that of a human foetus with curved thorax protected by the folded, tattered wings. I left it in its desolate repose and as I passed through the garden on my way to the house, I shook the lowest branch of the middle mountain ash tree so that in the silence, the crimson fruit, soft as it was, made a faint sound as it fell on the gravestone.

KATHLEEN TOOLE

a short space

ANGIE AND I were among the first ones in, running through the fine fall rain, and we found a table by the door. Angie took her seat and placed the plate of ice cream on the table. I set mine down and it bounced soggily. I was sorry I had come. Really I had no place here. I had been graduated the preceding June, cap, gown, tassle at the correct angle, diploma and all. Now my diploma lay between two pieces of cardboard in the bottom of my cedarchest at home.

The woman who had the field house concession was all sudden animation; she fluttered behind the counter as a duck does when surprised in a tight place. No doubt she had been sitting desultorily watching the reception on the green outside, which robbed her of business for the afternoon. Since it was hard for her to wedge herself through the swinging door that enclosed her she stood making small jerky gestures while everyone, students, professors, instructors, assistants, even the president and his wife came laughing and talking in a bewildered sort of way, bearing dishes of ice cream with little cakes balanced on their rims through the screen doors that slammed every time they were released, until there were no more tables and people stood against the walls.

Angie was speaking, but I could hear only her voice, indistinct, the words blurred. I leaned closer and watched her face. Suddenly she stopped and smiled. She had slightly protruding teeth over which her lips closed tightly, even when she smiled; this gave her face a determined and rather resentful air. I smiled back, but I felt foolish. I wished that when Angie had asked me I had made some quick adequate excuse.

Looking about, I saw them all. It was their duty to welcome the new students, and here they were. Covertly I glanced from table to table without finding the face I sought.

I might have known; it would not have done. I could visualize the sardonic smile, the blue eyes, so knowing, so aware, judging us all. Swiftly I searched Angie's face; she was eating her ice cream imperturbably. I had often marveled that, close as we were, she knew so little of what I felt.

There was Mr. Gordon, the professor of music; he was tall and very thin. His face looked like a caricature of some good kind sensitive face, with its drooping nose and round melancholy eyes. Somehow I had always felt sorry for him; I knew obscurely that he deserved better. There in a far corner sat the president and his wife. Her hat with its wide brim turned back created an illusion of youthfulness about the patient prettiness of her face. He talked and smiled; his mouth was grimly jovial. I could not see his eyes. Not far from us sat Mr. Taylor, the botany professor. Angie was his office assistant. He smiled pleasantly but she did not see him, and I smiled in return. Again I felt awkward and foolish. I had been in his office several times, but he hardly knew me. I looked quickly away.

The rain had ceased, the sun came out, the drops on the lush grass sparkled and flashed. A few people opened the screen doors and stepped outside. Upon those who remained within there settled one of those short periods of silence that sometimes fall upon groups of people. Some played with their paper spoons. One man was examining his fingernails. Others simply sat with their chins propped in their palms and gazed without.

Only some brash and slightly ridiculous soul possesses courage sufficient to break these silences. I waited, musing. Of course: Mrs. Pochez.

She sailed over to our table and sank in one of the chairs. It trembled with her weight.

"Hello, Angie, dear, how are you today?" she said rapidly. She postured a little and threw me a doubtful smile.

Angie smiled in return. "Mrs. Pochez, do you know—?"

"Oh yes, of course, how are you, my dear?" Her eyes traveled restlessly over the tables and returned to pause on me fleetingly in a stare of pure unrecognition. Then she resumed her scrutiny, saying, "I see we are all to welcome the dear new students." She gave Angie a sweet little smile. "All but our new sociology instructor, Mr.—ah, your neighbor, isn't he?"—though she very well knew his name. "Odd, I haven't glimpsed him this afternoon."

An avid look came into her eyes. "Have you girls seen him?"

"No, I haven't," Angie murmured. I did not answer at all. Though her glance was casual, I felt the color deepen in my face and throat.

"Is he ill perhaps?" Mrs. Pochez said speculatively. Her eyes rested momentarily, too brightly perhaps, on my face.

"I don't think so," Angie said.

"Ah well. Surely he must be ill. One should make friends with the sudents from the first. I don't think—" she broke off, as though reconsidering, and fixed us with her fleeting smile. Daintily she lifted her wrist and looked at her watch. "Well, good afternoon, girls, so nice to have seen you. I must be running along." She waved us a coy farewell.

I sat and made vicious little marks in the paper saucer with my paper spoon.

"All right," Angie said. "Don't mutilate the furniture. We'll go now." She rose, and I gathered my purse and gloves. She opened the screen door.

Behind us the people were already pushing back the frail chairs, balancing them when they swayed. They moved laughing and talking toward the doors. Once outside I started down an unfrequented walk.

"Wait a minute," Angie said. "Someone will give us a lift."

"Not me. Not today they won't." Then I added, "Please, Angie. Let's walk."

She hesitated, looking over her shoulder at the groups moving across the lawn.

"Oh, all right," she said, a trifle cross, for she disliked

walking. She said the broken sidewalks bruised her feet.

I thought as we walked along that this was no doubt true. Angie hated all broken useless things; she had no patience with things that did not fit. This feeling extended to people: she refused to understand people who had not found their proper place in the world. So there were moments when I felt uneasy in her presence. "What are you going to *do?*" she had a way of asking, her eyes flecked with a curious distrust. "Now that you're out of school you can't just sit."

I still did not have an answer.

We walked the rest of the way in silence. Her home was not far. As we turned in the walk, Jack ran to meet us. He was Angie's little brother, five years old, with straight yellow hair and a confidential manner.

"I got my rabbit," he cried. "I got my rabbit today!"

"You did," Angie said flatly. She went into the house.

"Umhum." He turned to me shyly. "You want to see him?"

"In a minute. Let me get my breath." I sat on the top step. He stood regarding me in silence. Finally, I roused myself and smiled. He smiled back, then his face changed, he looked at once adult and quizzical. He came close and whispered, "Come see."

I hesitated, struck by his expression. "Your rabbit?" I asked doubtfully. He grinned, at once conspiring and sly.

"Jist come on," he insisted. He took my hand and pulled me over in front of the house next door. He pointed to the porch.

"He's asleep," he said solemnly. He looked up in my

face, curious and expectant. "He's been asleep a long time."

It was the sociology professor. He lay stretched out in one of the lawn chairs, in absolute indolence, yet with a certain sleeping watchfulness. I had seen my cat, Napoleon, sleep like that many times.

Indeed, there always hovered some aura of the male cat about him, slow, insolent yet lithe, but you knew too how shadow-swift the raw young shoulders could spin about, the arm flash out, the hand snap shutter-tight.

I must have stared a second too long, for, stretching widely, he awoke. He spied us immediately.

"Hello," he drawled, and his lip pursed delicately under the clever little mustache. His eyes gleamed up from beneath the silky brows and when he looked at me it was as though someone showed his teeth in an even smile and shut the door quietly in my face.

Yielding to sudden impulse I turned away without replying and started down the walk toward home.

Let him think what he liked: that I was rude, ill-bred, or simply raw and young; what difference?

"My rabbit!" Jack cried out after me. "Don't you want to see my rabbit?"

I trudged along, pretending not to hear, not even bothering to skirt the puddles that had formed thinly in the worn pavement. Suddenly I stopped quite still, and standing there in the falling day I knew that his glance had not dismissed me because I was rude or ill-bred or even callow and young.

Sharp and clear as a flash-beam the realization came to me instead that he must have known and had to do with many kinds of women other than those whose every act shapes itself against a deliberate background—whether it be one of position, family, or wealth—women who move across the stage of life with their own particular backdrop painted in. What had he discovered as the source of this other, more important kind of self-assurance, I asked myself. I should like to know. It was a question which often returned to trouble me. How does one achieve it? I somehow thought of it as an extremely valuable possession which I lacked and which I coveted intensely. If it does not come from without it must spring from within, I reasoned. The thought occurred to me that perhaps the roots of this assurance feed on a definite knowledge of self, an acceptance, no, more, a love and possibly even a glorification of self. Vaguely I sensed in these quiet, self-possessed persons a continual gathering up and conserving of all forces and powers: no waste, nothing lost or scattered.

And I—

I had a vision of myself in oxfords and loose, ill-fitting sweater and skirt.

It had been toward the end of the second semester, one of those early spring days that begin cool and warm up quickly. The books I carried were heavy, cutting my arms and wrists, and I hurried to reach the comparative coolness of my next classroom. As I rounded the corner of the building I saw him; he was reading a letter, but I could not step aside quickly enough and we collided. My books tumbled to the ground.

"So sorry!" he exclaimed. "My fault!"

I did not deny it. I felt horribly embarrassed, standing there with my arms dangling while he bent down and gathered up the books. One had fallen open and the pages sprawled nakedly in the sun.

He rose and gave them to me, then stood dusting his hands and smiling. I felt my face burn red; the tips of my ears stung.

His eyes traveled over my face. The freshness went out of them and they veiled slightly.

"Where are you bound in such a hurry?" His tone mocked me gently.

"Nowhere," I murmured, somehow unable to meet his eyes.

"Quite a lot of books to carry on such a hot day."

"Oh, no," I said confusedly. "Not so many." In my self-consciousness I peered over as though I were counting them. "Only three." I began to edge off down the walk. His brows lifted a fraction and he smiled, momentarily pursing his lips; finally he turned and sauntered around the corner of the building.

And I—walking now through the fading day—I remembered my awkwardness and confusion, and how I had watched, with a shamed and fugitive greediness, his bent head and the hands gathering up the tumbled books.

During my four years in college I spent most of my class time in Science Hall. Approaching it down the wide, shaded walk I had often reflected that there was something hang-dog, pathetic about this long two-story brick structure, as though it had borne too much wind and weather, too much ivy had clung to its walls, the moss-hung trees had crept too near. It wore none of the traditional dignity of campus buildings, either inside or out;

indeed within it presented an aspect more abused and self-pitying than without. The very walls seemed to sag, the floors sloped unnaturally, the bannisters framing the stairs were grooved by time, dirt, and the passage of many hands.

Walking toward home, careful now to skirt the puddles, unaccountably it occurred to me that I need never, unless I chose, see that old building again, not in rain or sun or snow, not in happiness or sorrow—and then I recalled one day during the first part of the last semester. I was going a bit early to a class upstairs because I had missed my previous one. There were a few minutes until bell time. As I tiptoed down the hall the planks complained like querulous voices. In one of the classrooms a boy was saying in a clear, regretful tone, "I'm afraid you're wrong, sir."

Then I stopped, startled by the scorn, almost the bold anger in the voice replying behind the closed door.

"May I presume, Mr. Stewart, to ask the source of your information?"

"Why, yes, sir," the boy answered readily and politely. "It was the Encyclopædia Britannica, the reference you gave us at our last meeting."

The class tittered softly. No one spoke.

Then the instructor's voice, heavy with sarcasm, came through the door.

"May I apologize," he said elaborately, "to the entire class for this gross error on my part?"

There was a silence, as sudden and solid as a crowd's roar. It mounted like some dull hard tangible thing, like the body of a dark heavy bird, and beat against the ear-drums as a bird might beat against glass.

I was seized with a curiosity I could not resist. I crept to the door and opened it the smallest possible crack. The wind might have done it. His desk was directly in my line of vision; I could have seen his face had his head not been turned toward the window. His arms lay on the desk thrust straight out. He held in his left hand a piece of chalk; the fingers of his right hand tapped this gently. It was the only sound in the room. The line of his face, the brow and chin, were curiously severe and still. Unnatural and provocative, his face had long teased me: I felt that if I could but glimpse the eyes, the mouth, at last I could seize the answer to my unanswerable question.

And then, without warning, the knob slid from under my moist palm, the door glided away and swung arc-like in upon the assembled class. Like a wave their heads, light and dark, turned toward me; I stood staring—dumb-founded, stricken, mute, with my eyes fixed stubbornly upon his averted face. Almost instantly he turned too, with a quick, defensive movement. When his eyes met mine the color struck his face like an angry hand.

But then, like money in a gypsy's hands, his expression altered. With a suave, contemptuous movement he rose and stood with the tips of his fingers resting on the desk; the whiteness of his teeth gleamed and his eyes glittered blue and cold above the sudden ridges rippling along the sides of his face.

"Class dismissed," he said.

Abruptly I turned and fled.

Once out of the building I walked slowly, agitatedly beneath the trees. Suppose I had stood my ground, insolently; suppose I had forced him to pass me in the doorway, near my eyes, my hands—he should have had to speak.

What would he have said? Some trivial thing. No matter, in the end I would have faltered, I would have agreed, whatever he said, smiling uneasily beneath the watchful blue of his eyes, as careless of me, and as indifferent, as are the skies themselves.

And now, I thought, walking home beneath the last fingers of the September day, another school year has begun. The pale, youthful faces will gleam, hovering momentarily in the dark rooms over the dark, somber books. Innocence and ignorance, ignorance and innocence. Yes, there is too high a premium placed upon youth. "But I am not a child." We are children too long, we make a mock of childhood.

It is better to know, I thought bitterly, as the darkness sifted down to the corners of the fences and spread beneath the bushes and trees, it is better to comprehend the motives of others and of one's own self. I remembered his mouth, youthful and fresh, its tenderness concealed by the sly mustache, and the guarding eyes. I saw now that I had invested him with a strength and a purpose which he did not possess. Had he treated me as a child because he recognized in me his own weaknesses and felt compelled to deny them?

I felt humble and wretched. I thought of my activities during the past four years; how inane they seemed, like letters that have been handled and read so much that they have become childish and futile, almost silly. And oppressed by the feeling that these same activities awaited me—true enough, in altered guise, masked and varied, but the same—I vowed in an excess of rebellion, "No. I won't have them. Not for me!"

I thought of the idle summer behind me, when the sound of the telephone or the doorbell rang out like a summons—and when in the late afternoon I sat on the porch, or moved about the yard, or walked in the town, watching, ever warily watching the long green waves of time flowing past—and wondered, what sign have I awaited, what word, what gesture—

Have I waited for him to call me to him? Ah, no, for it was all no more than a delusion and his was but a face I had cajoled to fill my dream. And I have moved through it wordless and awkward, for I knew it was not real. Without ever having known reality or being told about it, I knew. And now, save for certain routine wrenchings of the truth, I was back—almost I had returned to the day when the small hand gripped the pencil and poised it to round out the first, the faltering A—A is for apple (an apple a day), B—B is for boy, C—C.

I had reached the river. My home lay in a modest suburb on the other side of this narrow stream. I paused on the bridge and stood gazing down at the water, bearing upon its austere surface the tidy debris of a summer day. And as I stood for a moment I fancied I glimpsed, staring back at me, defenseless and awry, the face of my first youth.

And in that instant, seeing my pale features glimmer and fade, I belonged neither to the past which folded itself like an accordion closed by quiet hands, nor to a future betrayed by circumstance, beset and confused by the cruel choice, but to that short space wherein all aspiration, all endeavor loomed potentially, nay, benignly assured, and lost in that fond dream, ignorant still, I turned and made my way toward home.

JESSAMYN WEST

the child's day

"I MINTA," the child said, "in the October day, in the dying October day." She walked over to the fireplace and stood so that the slanting sunlight fell onto her bare shoulder with a red wine stain. The ashes, so light and dry, smelled raw, rain-wet. Or perhaps it's the water on the chrysanthemums, she thought, or perhaps the bitter, autumn-flavored chrysanthemums themselves.

She listened for her second heart-beat, the three-day tap of the loosened shingle. But it was dead, it beat no more. For three days the Santa Ana had buffeted the house, but now at evening it had died down, had blown itself out. It was blown out, but it left its signs: the piled sand by the east door sills, the tumble weeds caught in the angle of the corral, the sign board by the electric tracks, face down; the eucalyptus upright, but with torn limb dangling.

"The Sabbath evening," said the girl, "the autumn Sabbath evening." And bright and warm against the day's sober death, the year's sad end, burned her own bright living.

She walked to her own room, across her fallen nightgown, past her unmade bed, and opened the casement window and leaned out toward the west. There the sun was near to setting, red in the dust, and the lights in the distant well riggings already blazed. She watched the sun drop until the black tracery of a derrick crossed its face.

"The day dies," murmured the girl; "its burnished wrack burns in yon western sky."

Then she was quiet so that no single word should fail to ripple the clear surface of her joy. The pepper tree rustled; there was a little stir in the leaves of the bougainvillaea. From the ocean, twenty miles away, the sea air was beginning to move back across the land. "It is as good against the dry face as water." She pushed her crackling hair away from her cheeks. "I won't have a wind break as thin even as one hair against my face."

She arched her bony chest under the tightly wrapped lace scarf, so that she could project as much of herself as possible into the evening's beauty. "Now the sun is down and the day's long dream ended. Now I must make the air whistle about my ears."

She came out of the long black lace scarf like an ivory crucifix—with a body no wider than her arms. Bloomers, slip, green rep dress on, and there she was—thirteen again, and the supper to get, and the house to clean. She had the supper in mind: a fitting meal for Sunday evening. Oyster soup. Oysters that actresses ate, floating in a golden sea of milk, and marble cup-cakes veined like old temples.

She had supper ready when the Duro turned into the

driveway bringing her family home from their drive—the cakes out of the oven, the milk just on for the soup.

"Well," said her father when he entered the room, "this is pretty nice." He walked over and held his hands to the fire. "Wood box full, too."

Her mother ran her finger over the top of the bookcase while she unwound her veil. "Minta, you'll burn us out dusting with kerosene."

Clenmie said, sniffing the air, "Did you bake me a little cake, Mintie?"

Minta watched the scarlet accordion pleating in the opening of her mother's slit skirt fan out as she held her foot toward the fire.

Father took off Clenmie's coat. "You should have gone with us, Minta. The wind's done a lot of damage over in Riverside County. Lost count of the roofs off and trees down."

"Is supper ready?" Mother asked.

"Soon as the milk heats, and I put the oysters in."

"Oyster soup!" exclaimed Father. "The perfect dish for a Sunday October evening. Did you get your studying done?" he asked curiously.

Minta nodded. Studying. Well, it was studying. There were her books and papers.

Father had said that morning before they left, "You're a bright girl, Minta. No need your spending a whole day studying. Do you more good to go for a ride with us."

"No, Father, I'm way behind." She could hardly wait until they left.

Finally at ten they got into the car, Mother on the front

seat close to Father, Clenmie behind. Father backed out of the driveway and a dusty swirl of wind caught Mother's scarlet veil. They waved her a sad good-by.

She had watched the red Duro out of sight, then turned and claimed the empty house for herself. She was as happy as a snail that expels the last grain of sand which has separated its sensitive fluid from its shell. Now she flowed back against the walls of her house in pure contentment. She stood stock still and shut her eyes and listened to the house sounds: first the dry, gusty breathing of the wind and the shingle's tap, then the lessening hiss of the tea kettle as the breakfast fire died, and the soft, animal pad of the rug as a slackening air current let it fall.

She opened her eyes. In the dining room the curtains lifted and fell with a summer movement in the autumn wind. She felt this to be perfect happiness: to stand in one room and watch in another the rise and fall of curtains. The egg-rimed dishes still stood on the uncleared breakfast table. She regarded the disorder happily. "Oh," she whispered, "it's like being the only survivor on an abandoned ship."

Stealthily she ran to lower all the blinds so that the room was left in yellow, dusty twilight. Then she made herself a fire of the petroleum-soaked refuse from the oil fields that they used for wood. When the oil began to bubble and seethe, and the flames darted up, black and red, she started her work.

She cleared the fumed-oak library table and ranged her books and papers precisely before her. Now her day began. Now she inhabited two worlds at once, and slid amphibian-like from one to the other, and had in each the best. She moved in Shelley's world of luminous mist, and emerged to hold her hand to the fire and to listen to the bone-dry sound of the wind in the palm trees.

She laid her hand across her open book feeling that the words there were so strong and beautiful that they would enter her veins through her palms and so flow to her heart. She listened to the wind and saw all the objects that bent before it: she saw the stately movement of dark tree tops, the long ripple of bleached, hair-like grass, the sprayed sea water, the blown manes of horses in open pasture, the lonely sway of electric signs along dusty main streets. "Far across the steppes," she said, "and the prairie lands, the high mesas and the grass-covered pampas." She watched the oil bubble stickily out of the wood and wondered how it seemed to feel again after these thousands of years the touch of the wind.

But this was dreaming, not doing her work. She opened her notebook to a half-filled page headed, "Beautiful, Lilting Phrases from Shelley." The list slid across her tongue like honey: "Rainbow locks, bright shadows, riven waves, spangled sky, aery rocks, sanguine sunrise, upward sky, viewless gale." She felt the texture of the words on her fingers as she copied them. The shingle tapped, the wind blew grittily across the pane, the fire seethed.

She finished Shelley and started on her own word list. She was through with the o's, ready to begin on the p's. She opened her old red dictionary. What words would she find here? Beautiful, strange ones? She looked ahead: pamero: a cold wind that sweeps over the pampas; parsalene: a mock moon; panada: bread crumbs boiled in milk;

picaroon: a rogue; pilgarlic: a baldheaded man; plangent: resounding like a wave. Her eyes narrowed and her cheek bones ached regarding this rich store.

She rolled her black, ribbed, gartered stocking back and forth across her knee and copied words and definitions. When she finished the q's she put her word notebook away and took out one called "The Poems of Aminta Eilertsen, Volume III." Each Sunday she copied one poem from her week's output into her poem book. Her poems were nothing like Shelley's. Shelley was beautiful, but he was not a modern. Minta was a modern, and when she wrote poetry she scorned the pretty and euphonious. This week's poem was called "You Do Not Have to Wipe the Noses of Your Dreams," and Minta thought it as stark and brutal as anything she had ever done. Slowly she copied it:

> "I was lithe and had dreams;
> Now I am fat and have children.
> Dreams are efflorescent,
> Dreams fade.
> Children do not.
> But then you do not have to
> Wipe the noses of your dreams."

"Yes," she said to her father, having remembered the poems, hers and Shelley's, the long list of words, "I finished my studying all right."

"Did anyone come while we were gone?" Mother asked.

"Mrs. Beal knocked, but she left before I got to the door."

She had scarcely moved from her table all morning. Now her back was stiff; she was cold and hungry. She put another petroleum-soaked timber on the fire and sat on the hassock warming her knees and eating her lunch: a mixture of cocoa, sugar and condensed milk as thick and brown as mud. She spooned it from gravy bowl to mouth and watched the murky flames and listened to the block of wood which was burning as noisily as a martyr. The oil seethed and bubbled like blood. She crouched on the hearth and heard behind the drawn curtains the hiss of sand against the windows. A current of air like a cold finger touched her cheek.

"What do I here," she wondered, "alone, abandoned, hiding?"

She pressed herself closely against the bricks and listened intently. She took a bite and let the sweet, brown paste slide down her throat so that no sound of swallowing should mask the approaching footfall, the heavy, guarded breathing. The room was filled with a noiseless activity. Well, she had known this would be her end. Soon or late they would come, search her out. In some such sordid, dirty, ill-lit hole as this she had been destined to make her end.

"In solitude and from this broken crockery, then, this last meal," she mused, and looked scornfully at the cracked bowl. "And those for whom the deed was done eat from crystal, on linen napery, and talk with light voices."

The wind had died down. But the curtains moved stealthily and the door into the hallway trembled a little in its frame. From somewhere in the house came the light click, click of metal on metal. Light, but continuous. She had not heard it before. She shifted her weight cautiously on the hassock so that she faced the room.

The wind came up again with a long, low, sick whistle; the shingle beat feverishly. She put down her bowl and started the search she knew must be made. She stepped out of her shoes and noiselessly opened the door into the hall. Cold, dark, and windowless it stretched the length of the house. Three bedroom doors opened off it, two to the west, one to the east. She searched the bedrooms carefully, though her heartbeat jarred her cheeks. She lunged against the long, hanging garments that might have concealed a hidden figure. She threw back the covers of the unmade beds. She watched the mirrors to see if from their silver depths a burning, red-rimmed eye might look into hers.

In Clenmie's room she finished her search. The loose shingle tapped like the heart of a ghost. Then she heard it: the sound she had been born to hear, the footstep her ears had been made to echo. Furtive footsteps: now fast, now slow, now pausing altogether. She leaned against the side of Clenmie's crib and waited for the steps to turn toward the house.

"But how could they know this was the house. What sign did I leave? What clew not destroy?"

The footsteps came on inexorably, turned out of the road onto the graveled walk, then proceeded quickly and resolutely to the front door. First there was a light, insistent knock, then the latched screen door was heavily shaken.

"He must have a force with him," Minta thought, "he is so bold," and waited for the crash of splintering boards, and braced her body for the thrust of cold steel that would follow. She thought fleetingly of Clenmie, and of her father and mother, and wondered if any sudden coldness about their hearts warned them of her plight.

The screen door shook again, and a woman's voice, old and quiet, called out, "Is there anyone there? I say, is there anyone home?" and ceased.

Slowly, cautiously Minta crept to the living room, lifted the side of the green blind. Old Mrs. Beal, her Sunday black billowing in the wind, was homeward bound from dinner with her daughter.

"I saw it was old Mrs. Beal on her way home from her daughter's," she told her father, giving him as much truth as she thought he could handle.

"Minta, you can get to the door fast enough when some of your friends are calling."

"I was busy," replied Minta with dignity. Her father looked at her doubtfully, but said no more.

Her mother combed out Clenmie's soft, white hair with her rhinestone back comb. "Did you forget to feed Brownie?" she asked.

"Of course I fed Brownie. I'll never forget her. She's my dearest friend."

Against the warm reality of Mrs. Beal's broad, homeward-bound back, the world that had been cold and full of danger dissolved. The dear room; her books, her papers; Clenmie's toys; mother's tissue cream on top of the piano; the fire sending its lazy red tongue up the chimney's black throat.

She stood warming herself, happy and bemused, like a prisoner unexpectedly pardoned. Then she heard again the click, click she had not recognized. Brownie at the back door!

"O poor Brownie, I forgot you. Poor kitty, are you hungry?" There was Brownie sitting on the back step, with fur blown and dusty, patiently waiting to be let in and fed. She was a young cat, who had never had a kit of her own, but she looked like a grandmother. She looked as if she should have a gingham apron tied around her waist, and spectacles on her nose, and now out of her grandmother's eyes she gave Minta a look of tolerance. Minta snatched the cat up and held her close to her face, and rubbed her nose in the soft, cool fur. When she got out the can of condensed milk she put Brownie by the fire and poured the milk into the bowl from which she had eaten her own lunch. Brownie lapped the yellow arc as it fell from can to bowl.

Minta crouched on the hearth with her eyes almost on a level with Brownie's. It was blissful, almost mesmeric to watch the quick, deft dart of the red tongue into the yellow milk. Her own body seemed to participate in that darting, rhythmic movement and was lulled and happy. "It is almost as if she rocked me, back and forth, back and forth, with her tongue," mused Minta.

When Brownie finished eating, Minta took her in her arms, felt the soft little body beneath the shaggy envelope of cinnamon fur. She lay on the floor close to the fire and cradled Brownie drowsily. Suddenly she kissed her. "My darling, my darling," she said, and caressed the cat the length of its long, soft body. Her hand tingled a little as it passed over the little pin-point nipples.

Some day her mother would tell her the secret phrase,

the magic sentence—something the other girls already knew. Then the boys would notice her. Then he would come. Ellen and Margaret and Phyllis already had notes from boys, and candy hearts on Valentine's day, and a piece of mistletoe at Christmas time. The boys rode them on their handle bars and showed them wrestling holds, and treated them to sodas. "But no one," she mourned, "ever looks at me." She pressed her apricot-colored hair close to the cat's cinnamon fur. "It's because mother hasn't told me yet. Something the other girls know. Sometime she'll tell me—some beautiful word I've been waiting a long time to hear. Then I'll be like a lamp lighted, a flower bloomed. Maybe she'll tell me tomorrow—and when I walk into school everyone will see the change, know I know. How will they know? My lips, my eyes, a walk, a gesture, the movement of my arms. But there's not a boy here I'd have, but someone far away, no boy. He will come and we will walk out along the streets hand in hand and everyone will see us and say, 'They were made for each other.' His hair will be like fur, soft and sooty black, and on his thin brown cheek will be a long, cruel scar. He will say, 'Kiss it, Minta, and I will bless the man who did it.' Ah, we shall walk together like sword and flower. All eyes will follow us and the people will say, 'This is Minta. Why did we never see her before?' "

Fire and wind were dying. Brownie slept on her arm. "He will come, he will come." Minta lifted Brownie high overhead, then brought her down sharply and closely to her breast.

"He will come, he will come." She kissed Brownie fiercely and put her on the floor, and ran to her mother's room, undressing as she went. She stepped out of her serge skirt and threw her Norfolk jacket across the room and sent her bloomers in a flying arc. She knew what she wanted. She had used it before—mother's long, black lace fascinator. She wound it tightly about herself from armpits to thighs. She unbraided her hair and let it hang across her shoulders. Then she turned to the mirror. "I have a beautiful body," she breathed, "a beautiful, beautiful body."

And because she regarded herself, thinking of him, him who was yet to come, it was as if he too saw her. She loaned him her eyes so that he might see her, and to her flesh she gave this gift of his seeing. She raised her arms and slowly turned and her flesh was warm with his seeing. Somberly and quietly she turned and swayed and gravely touched now thigh, now breast, now cheek, and looked and looked with the eyes she had given him.

She moved through the gray dust-filled room weaving an ivory pattern. Not any of the dust or disorder of her mother's room fazed her, not its ugliness or funny smell. Hair bubbled out of the hair receiver, the stopper was out of the Hoyt's cologne bottle, the mirror was spattered with liquid powder. She made, in her mind, a heap of all that was ugly and disordered. She made a dunghill of them and from its top she crowed.

"The curtains, green as vomit, and hanging crooked, the gray neckband on the white flannel nightgown, the dust on the patent leather shoes, I hate them and dance them down. Nothing can touch me. I am Minta. Or I can dance with them," and she clasped the sour-smelling nightgown to her and leaped and bent. "This is evil, to be naked, to like the feel of gritty dust under my feet, the bad smell, the dim light."

She regarded her face more closely in the spattered mirror. "There is something wanton and evil there," she thought, "something not good. Perhaps I shall be faithless," and she trembled with pity for that dark one who loved her so dearly. She shook back her hair and pressed her cool hands to her burning cheeks and danced so that the dust motes in the slanting shaft of light shot meteor-like, up and down.

"I can dance the word," she whispered, "but I cannot say it." So she danced it, wrapped in the black fascinator, with the dust motes dancing about her. She danced it until she trembled and leaning on bent elbows looked deep into the mirror and said, "There is nothing I will not touch. I am Minta. I will know everything."

All at once she was tired. She turned and walked slowly to the living room. Brownie lay by the dead fire. "I, Minta," she had said, "in the October day, in the dying October day," and turned to do the evening work.

"If the milk boils your soup will be spoiled," Mother said. "We've been here long enough for it to heat."

"Yes, Sister, let's eat," said Father, "it's been a long day."

"Yes, let's eat," cried Minta. "It's been a long, beautiful day," and she ran to the kitchen to put the oysters in the milk.

YVOR WINTERS

the brink of darkness

LATE IN October the first snow had come, large heavy flakes with shaggy edges, far apart, moving down in vast circles from a soft sky. The trees in the orchard outside the window of the dining-room were hard and cold, and shone like smooth rock against the earth and the colorless air. And the big rough flakes moved cautiously among them, here and there, as if exploring the terrain. There was a slight flurry, and the flakes gathered faster; then followed flurry upon flurry, a few moments apart, a steady slow pulsation, and with each the air was whiter and darker; till at last, the flurries coming imperceptibly closer and closer together, the air was an unbroken sheet of snow through which one could hardly move, the flakes were small and quick, and darkness, amid the confusion, had superseded twilight.

During the winter months the snow had lain deep over the rounded hills, and I had gone out on skis with my two Airedales. The clouds were of a soft even gray, and they seemed to have no lower edges, so that the sky had no identity—there was merely the soft air. The snow merged into the air from below with no visible dividing line. Often I should not have known whether I was going uphill or down, had it not been for the pull of gravity and the visible inclination of the skis. Often I came to the top of a rise and started down with no warning save the change in speed, or arrived at the bottom of a hill with no warning save the sudden slowing. I could travel for miles and see only one or two houses. Sometimes a mouse appeared, floundering as if in heavy air, and the dogs would lunge clumsily after it, snap it up, and drop it dead, leaving a small spot of blood suspended in grayness; but the few rabbits were better equipped and evaded them.

Once I passed a small pen made of chicken-wire, behind a barn, a pen in which there were fifteen or eighteen yearling coyotes. The farmers often captured the cubs during the spring plowing, and kept them into the next winter in order to slaughter them for the fur. These were about ready for killing. They swung in a group to the fence as I passed, lifting the foreparts of their bodies swiftly and gently, to drop them precisely facing, their shoulders flat, the front legs straight and close together, the wide sharp ears erect, the narrow little noses examining the air detail by detail. It was strange that they never broke through so slight a fence, yet there they were; young dogs would have torn through it with scarcely a pause, scarcely the sense of an obstacle. But these creatures were innocent and delicate, spirits impeded by a spell, puffs of smoke precise at the tips. As I passed, they turned their heads, watching me, then moved away and apart, to lie down in the snow or crawl under their small shelter. They had been the only sign of life amid four hours of snow, and they had made no sound. They had focused upon me for a moment their changing, shadowy curiosity, and then had been dissipated as if by the quiet of the hills.

I remembered the preceding fall. The three of us, myself and the Stones, had been puzzled by the luminosity of the stubble at night. On the slope south of the house, even on moonless nights, it had a curious glow, a kind of phosphorescence, that appeared to light the air for a few inches above the ground and then to stop suddenly. When the moon was full, the glow for several feet above the fields was so dense that the eye could scarcely penetrate to the ground. At a definite level above the field the glow stopped suddenly, and one could look for miles through watery moonlight over hills that seemed smothered in soft fire. The dogs, running through the fire, below the height of visibility, were dark vortices, blurred and shapeless, stirring rapidly in the motionless flame. Above the roof of the house, in the cold nights of late autumn, Orion, the Pleiades, and all the bright powder of the northern heaven, moved steadily from east to west; and the Great Dipper, low to the north, with few stars near it, its large stars plain and heavy, moved with an equal and compensatory pace from west to east and slipped in behind one of the hills.

In spite of the bright autumn and the shadowy winter, the village had been an unbearable blaze of heat in June. The winter wheat, which had germinated and grown eight or ten inches high under the snow, had shot up prodigiously in the spring warmth. The round hills were green, for even the spring crop was well along. The tall elms were in leaf; the apricot orchard about the house was heavy and dark; each tree was a black void growing shadowy and visible at the edges. The summer beat on the ground with no motion. The two white goats across the road lay panting in the shade, trembling watery blotches, barely discernible.

Once the Stones went up into the mountains for the afternoon, taking me with them. The mountains were only ten miles back of the village, and on the way we stopped at a farm owned by Mr. Stone and leased to a family of Seventh Day Adventists. The Stones wanted to get the girl of the family to come and help with the housework. She came to the gate with a shovel and a bucket as we drove up, a tall coarse-boned person, somewhere between twenty-five and thirty-five, with sharply drooping and very long shoulders and a small face, snub-nosed and almost featureless, her mouth open. She looked like one who had been intensely preoccupied, and who had discovered us suddenly. She was sweaty and had dust on her clothes and was visibly panting. She promised to come.

During January and the first week in February, the weather was extremely cold. The kitchen range was red hot, and so was the stove in the dining-room, but the corners of the rooms were never warm enough, and in the halls you could always see your breath. I kept my stove on the second floor as hot as I dared, and I usually sat up till one and two in the morning to keep the fire from dying down, for no bed-clothes were adequate. One night the mercury fell to sixty below zero. During this cold spell Mrs. Stone took to her bed, become suddenly very weak. She had always been frail; it appeared now that out of humility and consideration for others she had been concealing her weakness till she had arrived at the point where concealment was impossible. Her strength ebbed very rapidly, and as the cold began to grow less savage, she suddenly died.

The undertakers were not allowed to remove her body from the house, for she had not wished it. They came and went. The nurse, a tall, gray-haired woman, asked me to bed the dogs in the barn for a few nights, for the body was to be placed in the hall at the foot of the stairs. The casket was wheeled in, when the undertakers had gone, a soft gray affair, with some sort of lacy material supported above it and dropping away on either side in the form of a tent. From within came the heavy odor of hot-house flowers; as the casket moved, the slight stiff shifting of the body was just visible through the curtain.

Asa Stone, who lived on a neighboring farm, took his father away for the night. The old man, in spite of his bulk, seemed shrunken; his face, pale and lifeless, fell away in heavy lines, and he seldom looked up. Asa led him by the arm to keep him from stumbling.

A neighbor woman came in to sit up with the nurse and myself. The three of us went into the hall and drew back the curtain from the casket. She was dressed in white, her head surrounded by lilies of the valley, her hair, in spite of her sixty years, pure black against the flowers. As we moved the casket a little, there was again the slight stiff shifting of the body. The face was very firm. The jaw was strong, almost too strong for a woman, had it not seemed a strength employed to achieve gentleness. The mouth, wide in proportion to the jaw, suggested her slight smile, but it was not smiling. It was finished. It seemed to have come to an ultimate balance, to have found itself. We dropped the curtain and returned to the dining-room.

Toward morning I went upstairs to lie down for a few hours, for I had to teach during the day. I came down about seven, passed the coffin in the first gray of the dawn, moved through the motionless cold, which seemed to be gathering heavier about it and which was somehow identified with the thin sweet odor, perhaps the odor of death, perhaps of the flowers, of which the casket itself, with its frosty tent, might have been the visible core.

At noon I returned. As I opened the door into the darkened hall, the casket awaited me, the sweet odor deepening on the still air. I was a trifle sickened; it affected me like the smell of ether. I had lunch and returned to my teaching. The casket awaited me in the darkness at five o'clock. In the dining-room the two women were talking and sometimes laughing as they got supper ready. I went up to my room and lay down but could not sleep. I was beginning to shudder a little as I passed the body, yet it was not from fear of the dead. The ghost, if she stood there waiting beside the body, fixing in memory the house in which she had lived for so many years and which she must now leave forever, was too patient, too gentle, to be feared. The thought of her inexpressible solitude filled me with pity.

On the morning after the third night the family began to gather for the funeral. Alvin, the younger son, and his wife, were the first to come, their features obscured with sorrow. Asa and Clara came with Mr. Stone between them; the children would be brought over later. Asa's features were those of his mother, but somehow smaller and harder, and with none of her serenity. He was a man who was seldom still for long, who seemed to know little of peace, whether of body or of spirit.

Asa and Clara moved the casket into the parlor and took away the veil. Soon the florist arrived, and I helped him bank the flowers.

In the kitchen there were coffee and a light breakfast for those who needed them. I went out for a cup of coffee. As I entered the kitchen, the Adventist girl from the country came in, her great awkward shoulders drooping and swinging as she moved, her eyes red. Her brother came behind her. He had been deformed from birth. He was over six feet tall, a man of great power and agility, but without forearms; where his elbows should have been, there were thick, red, wrinkled wrists, and on each wrist there were two long red fingers without nails. His nose was long and coarse, and his voice was nasal. To make up for the shortness of his arms, he had developed violent but agile motions of the upper body; doing even the simplest things, he seemed the victim of some unhappy and uncontrollable agitation. He was a teamster by trade, when he had time from his farm, and he often worked for Asa. His abnormality had made him an exile from human society, and as a result he had acquired an unusual sympathy for horses and mules, with whom he could accomplish extraordinary things, and that part of his nature which was not satisfied by this companionship had turned to religion. When driving a team, he sang in a loud nasal drone, almost devoid of variation, hymns which he intended merely to quiet his own spirit, but which, on a still day, could be heard among the hills for a mile or more. He sat at the kitchen table now, as I drank my coffee, his large bony trunk darting suddenly this way and that, his wrinkled fingers squirming about a piece of bread or a knife, his sharp mouth dropping pious ejaculations between swallows. "Eli can sure talk religion," Asa had once said of him with admiration.

At the church I sat with the family, in a private room to the side of the pulpit. After the sermon I looked once more into the casket. The black hair seemed not to have stirred. The face was not heavily wrinkled, but there were a few small wrinkles about the mouth and eyes. The skin was preternaturally and evenly white, and in the wrinkles there seemed a trace as of an underlying darkness, even and impenetrable. At the grave, a mile and a half outside of town, the ceremonies were brief, for a vile sleet had set in. The coffin was lowered; the last prayer was read; and the grave was filled with stones and mud. As we drove away, I looked back to see a huge mound of hot-house flowers, dark heavy green, and clear hard white and yellow, lying as if murdered in the colorless air, beneath driving sleet.

That afternoon Alvin and Asa began moving the furniture from the lower part of the house. Two days later they had finished. I was to keep my rooms in the upper part till the house should be sold, since there were only a few months left till the summer vacation. The old man would stay with Alvin. That was late in February. A few days later another heavy freeze set in.

I made no attempt to keep the lower part of the house

warm, although I had to use it occasionally. It was absolutely bare. Even the curtains and window-blinds were gone, and when I went down to the kitchen at night for a glass of water, or crossed the parlor and kitchen to reach the basement for coal, I moved through a naked glare of electric light, with wide bare windows on two sides of me, my feet echoing, my hands stiff with the cold. I came to see myself moving in this room, as if from the outside, and I sometimes wondered who I was. When I came home at dusk from teaching and entered the lower hall, I thought I could still feel the earthy cloud at its center. Sometimes my flesh went chill. I came gradually to carry more and more coal upstairs every morning, and soon I was getting enough to last me through the night. Upstairs were the dogs and the stove; below was the echoing desolation.

During the three nights that Mrs. Stone had lain below me in the hall, my sensitivity to death, to the obscure and the irrelevant, had been augmented. I felt that I saw farther and farther into the events about me, that I perceived a new region of significance, even of sensation, extending a short distance behind that of which I had always been aware, suggesting the existence of far more than was even now perceptible. This might have unnerved me had it not been for the firmness of the woman in the coffin. In her were united the familiar and the inchoate. The certainty of her expression gave me pause. She was like a friend bidding me be quiet with raised hand, a friend whose bidding I could trust to be authoritative. But with her departure there remained only the demonic silence which she had introduced, and to which for three nights she had given coherence and a meaning.

The dogs, large and unkempt, a mother and her son, were old enough to enjoy spending most of their time on my bed in the cold weather. When I came up the stairs, they would be waiting, their heads on their paws, their faces expressing an identical gentle question. I had kept their bed in another room at first, but the cold had forced me to close the room, and I was glad enough to have the two sleep with me. The field mice from round about were invading the empty building in greater and greater numbers. They were too quick for the dogs at close quarters, especially on the second floor, where there was still a good deal of furniture. The mice lost all fear, and the dogs no longer disturbed them, but would lie still for half an hour, regarding the scratching, shadowy little creatures with indifferent curiosity or remote amusement. During the first week in March, while the cold spell still endured, the dogs did not come one morning when I called them as I was about to leave the house. Nor did they come the next day nor the next. I knew well enough what had happened, and I would not have been greatly troubled had it not been for the weather and a few porcupines in a small wood lot several miles away. Every afternoon I walked over the hills, trying to get a sight of them on the snow. A light snow had fallen after their going, and their tracks had been covered. I did not know how long it might take them to find their way in from among the hills. Here and there a farmer had seen them. They had been living for several days on the offal of a slaughtered calf and had been sleeping in haystacks. Several farmers had tried to catch them for me, but the dogs were powerful, and, when in trouble, as suspicious and nearly as dangerous as wolves.

They seemed to be moving in a wide circle, which I gradually mapped, but on which I never intercepted them. If I didn't meet them, at least it was only a question of time till they would pick up my trail and follow me in. The hills were a cold thin blue, darker where the wind had riffled the snow and the earth showed through, their edges definite against the sky with a cold hair-line precision. There were no clouds, and as I returned home at dusk, a few small white stars appearing, the sky stood above me unvaulted, a steely gray, without distance or dimension.

While the dogs were gone, I spent as much of my nights as I could in reading, and when I could no longer read, I took to watching the mice. At first they had seemed to me uncanny, but gradually I came to be fond of them. I put out food for them, and sometimes a dish of milk. With their food they were likely to be boisterous, snatching it and running off, or throwing it about in play if they were not hungry; with their drink they were delicate and gentle, advancing to the rim of the saucer like far-away gazelles, the natives of this dissolving wilderness, their feet as sensitive as ants, their round eyes rolling quickly this way and that.

One night after I had been watching the mice without moving for nearly an hour, I got up suddenly and went downstairs for a glass of water. The sound of my feet rang out with tremendous volume as I descended the stair; as I crossed the glare of the front room, the echo seemed to resound from the room above, as if I were walking up there. I stood still to quiet the noise. I was alone and erect, a few feet from the broad window, bright emptiness behind me. The light from the window fell on the snow outside. It had been warm enough at noon for a slight glaze to form. The shape of the light on the glaze was sharp-edged and clear. Only, at the upper left-hand corner of the window there was darkness, a tangle of withered vines outside. I stared at the smooth surface of the snow thus suddenly revealed to me, like a new meaning not divisible into any terms I knew. Again I had the illusion of seeing myself in the empty room, in the same light, frozen to my last footprints, cold and unmeaning. A slight motion caught my eye, and I glanced up at the darkened corner of the window, to be fixed with horror. There, standing on the air outside the window, translucent, a few lines merely, and scarcely visible, was a face, my face, the eyes fixed upon my own. I moved on quickly to the kitchen; the reflection started and vanished.

The next morning, upon reaching my office, I heard of the catastrophe of the night before. One of my students, the son of one of my colleagues, a boy who was to have graduated this spring but who had been confined to the pest-house with meningitis, had, in the night, while no nurse was present, been seized with delirium, had leapt from his bed and escaped from the door of the hospital in his night-clothes. He had run the four blocks separating the hospital and his home, had broken a window and climbed in. An hour later, at midnight, his parents had returned, to find him sitting before a smoldering fireplace in an icy house, moaning to be taken to his room. He had never regained consciousness; before morning he was dead.

There was another funeral in the Presbyterian church. This time the coffin was kept closed, from respect for the disease. The coffin was banked high behind and on either end with yellow chrysanthemums. The boy's fraternity came in a body, twenty and some boys seated in two front rows at one side, looking curiously young and helpless before the coffin. The waxen petals of the chrysanthemums glowed in the dusk of the church; they seemed almost to move, curling and uncurling ever so little. There was something innocent and pathetic about the flowers, these earthy blossoms, cut clean from the ground from which they had struggled, foaming dimly, still dimly alive in the gloom, struggling imperceptibly, curling imperceptibly inward, as if they were the sluggish dead incarnate, dying slowly again in pity, returning numbly to the earth.

At the end of four days, toward nightfall, the bitch returned, emaciated and limping, her head and throat, inside and out, completely covered with quills, her mouth forced open with the mass of them, her tongue hanging out, swollen, and white with quills as far back as I could see. I was prepared for this kind of return. I held her and poured vinegar over the entire wounded area, to soften the quills. She screamed, but lay still. Had it been the other dog, I would have sent for help and for morphine; I knew that morphine would only make the bitch stupidly savage without calming her, even in doses so large as to be dangerous. I sat astride her body, letting my entire weight fall on her ribs to hold her down. She tossed this way and that, screaming, her mouth foaming with blood. It was strange how hard the things wedged themselves into the cartilage: sometimes I had to pull several times before I could loosen one, and it would come out followed by a gush of blood. The light on the floor was poor and the work was hard; at the end of two hours I was exhausted almost to numbness.

The bitch was panting and weak; sometimes she moaned feebly; the floor was spattered with blood for three or four feet around; but she was clean of visible quills, and few seemed to have buried themselves. I washed her with disinfectant, poured a drink of warmish water into her mouth, and turned her loose. She staggered feebly to her feet and walked over and lay down on the rug behind the stove. The inner surface of her mouth was devoid of membrane, was a bloody pulp, and her head was a clotting spongy mass. It had happened before, and she would survive it; we both of us knew it; she moved her tail feebly, and then cautiously laid her head on her paws. In the morning some boys led the other dog in staggering; they had found him late the night before in the same condition as the bitch, and had taken him to a veterinary before bringing him home.

For the next week most of my free time was spent in nursing the dogs; my bed cover and my rugs were stained with blood; the corners of the room accumulated deeper and deeper dust; the dust lay under the bed in soft whorls; I was busy and very tired and slowly lost the habit of noticing. Once near the end of March, some friends of the Stones from the next town stopped by to see the old man. I explained his absence, and asked them in for a cup of coffee. They came in dubiously, a tall silent old farmer and his gray small wife, the two of them troubled by the combination of my books, of my general affability, and of the dire squalor in which I lived. The dogs sniffed them curiously, extending their raw and scabious heads, and I sent them back to the bed. The old people finally took their leave with great formality.

During the first week in April, Alvin appeared at the door to say that the house had been sold and that the new owner wished to take possession as soon as possible. I arranged for the room across the street and began to move at once. A Chinook had begun the day before Alvin's appearance and continued for three days; it was the last thaw of the season. On most of the hills the winter wheat was already high, and the hills lay green as the snow vanished. Far across the valley I could hear the puffing of a tractor, and now and then I could see the tiny iron thing crawling rapidly in straight lines across the hills, appearing and disappearing suddenly and in unlikely ways, leaving black earth behind.

Now my belongings were moved, and I would stay in the new house until early June. My new landlord was a teamster with seven children and a tired wife. I should not be with them long enough to become acquainted. The children swarming about the little house bothered me, but I liked them well enough in a way; they were a part of the season. Just outside my door was an old phonograph, which one of the older girls played incessantly. The grass was already green under my new window; the trees were in bud; the two white goats would kid in a week, and the kids, bloody and tottering at first, would be within a few days leaping here and there in the cold shadows, balancing and spinning on a single foot, front or rear, it mattered little, nipping buds they would not care to eat, trying to make friends with the dogs, to the patient embarrassment of the dogs and the consternation of their mothers.

I thought back over the past months, of the manner in which I had been disturbed, uncentered, and finally obsessed as by an insidious power. I remembered that I had read somewhere of a kind of Eastern demon who gains power over one only in proportion as one recognizes and fears him. I felt that I had been the victim of a deliberate and malevolent invasion, an invasion utilizing and augmenting to appalling and shadowy proportions all of the most elusive accidents of my life, my new penumbra of perception thus rendering to what would otherwise have appeared the contingent the effect of coherent and cumulative meaning. Finally, through some miscalculation on the part of the invader, or through some other accident, I had begun to recover the limits of my old identity. I had begun this recovery at the time of the immersion in the brute blood of the bitch. The invading power I could not identify. I felt it near me still, but slowly receding.

I got up from where I sat and stretched myself out in the sun. I was minutely aware of my movements, my inclinations, my bodily functions. I could not blink my eyes without being conscious of the darkness; I knew I was tired. It was as if there were darkness evenly underlying the brightness of the air, underlying everything, as if I might slip suddenly into it at any instant, and as if I held myself where I was by an act of the will from moment to moment. From far over the hills I heard a low snoring drone, rising and falling, as if it came from a lonely bull in a far pasture. A quick and powerful team, four abreast, and drawing a wheel plow, came over the rise at the distance of a quarter of a mile. The plow came down the slope swiftly and started around the base of the hill to circle slowly upward again, the horses arching and rippling, the driver bending forward and moving rapidly here and there to urge them on. From the sound and from the strange movements of the driver, I recognized Eli. I lay back and closed my eyes. The sun poured steadily into me. In a month I should be leaving for Colorado. I would never return.

JANET LEWIS

the wife of martin guerre

FOREWORD

The history of the wife of Martin Guerre is one of those tales in which the truth is so remarkable that it can hardly be believed. I do not know whether the original documents pertaining to the case are still available at Toulouse. Phillips, whose works were, during the early years of the nineteenth century, the standard English authority on the rules of evidence, transcribed the case in one of his discussions of circumstantial evidence, giving the details very fully, and the facts, however strange, bequeathed us by so eminent a jurist can hardly be discredited. The rules of evidence vary from century to century and country to country, and the morality which compels many of the actions of men and women varies also, but the capacities of the human soul for suffering and for joy remain very much the same.

I. ARTIGUES

One morning in January, 1539, a wedding was celebrated in the village of Artigues. That night the two children who had been espoused to one another lay in bed in the house of the groom's father. They were Bertrande de Rols, aged eleven years, and Martin Guerre, who was no older, both offspring of rich peasant families as ancient, as feudal and as proud as any of the great seignorial houses of Gascony. The room was cold. Outside the snow lay thinly over the stony ground, or, gathered into long shallow drifts at the corners of houses, left the earth bare. But higher, it extended upward in great sheets and dunes, mantling the ridges and choking the wooded valleys, toward the peak of La Bacanère and the long ridge of Le Burat, and to the south, beyond the long valley of Luchon, the granite Maladetta stood sheathed in ice and snow. The passes to Spain were buried under whiteness. The Pyrenees had become for the winter season an impassable wall. Those Spaniards who were in French territory after the first heavy snowfall in September, remained there, and those Frenchmen, smugglers or soldiers or simple travelers who found themselves on the wrong side of the Port de Venasque were doomed to remain there until spring. Sheep in fold, cattle in the grange, faggots heaped high against the wall of the farm, the mountain villages were closed in enforced idleness and isolation. It was a season of leisure in which weddings might well be celebrated.

Bertrande had not spoken to Martin in all her life until that morning, although she had often seen him; indeed she had not known until the evening before that a marriage had been arranged. That morning she had knelt with Martin before his father and then had walked with him across the snow, dressed bravely in a new red cape and attended by many friends and relatives and by the sound of violins, to the church of Artigues where the marriage ceremony had been completed. She had found it quite as serious an affair as first communion.

Afterwards, still to the music of the violins, which sounded thin and sharp in the cold air, she had returned to the house of her husband where a huge fire of oak logs garnished with vine-trimmings roared in the big fireplace, and where the kitchen, the principal room of the house, was set with improvised tables, long boards laid over trestles. The stone floor had been freshly strewn with broken boughs of evergreen. The sides and bottoms of the copper pans flashed redly with the reflection of the flames, and the air was rich with the good smell of roasting meat and of freshly poured wine. Underfoot the snow from the sabots melted and sank beneath the trodden evergreens. A smell of humanity and of steaming wool mingled with the odors of the food, and the room was incredibly noisy with conversation.

It was a gay, an important event. Everyone was intensely jubilant, but the small bride received very little attention. After the first embraces and compliments, she sat beside her mother at the long table and ate the food which her mother served her from the big platters. Now and again she felt her mother's arm steal warmly about her shoulders, and felt herself pressed briefly against her mother's breast, proudly and reassuringly, but as the feast proceeded her mother's attention became more engrossed with the conversation of the curé, who sat opposite, and of the groom's father, who sat upon her other side, and Bertrande, immune from observation in the midst of all this commotion which was ostensibly in her honor, looked about the room at her ease, and fed pieces of hard bread dipped in grease to the woolly Pyrenean sheep dog with the long curly tail who nosed his head into her lap from his place beneath the table. By and by, when the dishes of soup and roast had given way to the boiled chestnuts, cheese, honey and dried fruits, she slipped from her place and began quietly to explore the room.

Behind the table where she had been sitting the beds were ranged, end to end, the curtains of yellow serge drawn close, each one an apartment in itself. The child brushed between these curtains and the stout backs of the merrymakers, moving slowly toward the nearer corner of the room, where she stood, her back against a tall cupboard, and surveyed the scene. Across from her the blackened fireplace occupied at least a third of the wall, and the brightness of the leaping flames left the corners on either side in confused semi-darkness. In the middle of the wall to the right, however, she spied a door, and toward that she gradually made her way. It proved to be the entrance to a long cold corridor, from which doors opened into storerooms, rooms for the shepherds, and lighted only by a small window of which the wooden shutters were closed. Another person had taken refuge from the festivities in this corridor, and was intent upon undoing the bolts of the shutters. The half of the shutter folded back, a flood of sharp snowy sunlight fell into the corridor, and in its brightness she recognized Martin. She made a step forward, uncertainly, and Martin, hearing it, turned and advanced upon her, his hands outstretched and a fearsome expression on his long, young face. He had disliked being married, and, in order to express his dislike of the affair, and also to express the power of his newly acquired sovereignty, he cuffed Bertrande soundly upon the ears, scratched her face and pulled her hair, all without a word. Her cries brought a rescuer, her mother's sister, who rebuked the bridegroom and led the bride back into the kitchen, where she remained beside her mother until the hour when she was led by her mother and her mother-in-law into the Chamber, the room on the opposite side of the kitchen, where stood the master's bed, now dedicated to the formalities of the wedding.

Bertrande was disrobed and attired in night garments and a bonnet-de-nuit. Martin was brought in and similarly attired, and the two children were put to bed together in the presence of all the company. In deference to the extreme youth of the bridal couple, however, the serge curtains were not pulled, and a torch, fastened to the wall, was left blazing.

The company remained in the room for a time, laughing at jokes of a time-honored nature, while the two children lay very still and did not look at each other. By and by the merrymakers drifted into the kitchen, and last of all the father of Martin Guerre paused in the doorway to wish his children a formal goodnight. Bertrande saw his features, exaggerated in the flare of the torch, bent in an expression of great seriousness, and the realization that henceforth her life lay beneath his jurisdiction came suddenly and overwhelmingly to the little girl. The door closed behind him. The unglazed window was also closed, but between the leaves of the shutter a draft came which shook the flame of the torch. Otherwise the air was still and dead. The floor was bare, and the room was unfurnished save for a row of carved chests against the wall and the great bed in which she lay. She was tired and frightened. She did not know what Martin might not take it into his head to do to her. Presently she felt him stir.

"I am tired of all this business," he said, turning on his side and burrowing his head into his pillow. Soon his breathing became regular, and, without daring to move her body, Bertrande relaxed. She was safe. Her husband was asleep.

From her high pillow she watched the torch, as the flame wavered, and little particles of blazing lint detached themselves and fell, smoking, to the stone floor. One was long in falling; it clung, a blazing thread, making the flame of the torch irregular and smoky. Then it too dropped. The warmth of the flock bed began to enclose the small thin body in something like security, a feeling almost as good as that of being home again. The light of the torch seemed to go out. The child began to doze.

An hour or so later the door opened and a large figure entered, substantially clothed in ample folds of brown wool and coifed in white linen, and bearing a tray; and crossed with leisured tread to the bedside. Whether it was merely the sense of being observed, or whether the stone floor had resounded or the silver rattled a little on the tray, Bertrande awoke and, opening her eyes, looked up into the square, benevolent face and the pleasant brown eyes of a woman whom she recognized dimly as a part of the house of Guerre. But it was not the face of her mother-in-law, no, it was the face of the servant who had stood at the doorway as the bridal party had returned from the church.

"You are awake. That is well," said the woman, smiling. "I warrant, if the boy were eight years older he would not be sound asleep at such an hour."

She rested the tray on the bed, and, reaching across the body of Bertrande, shook Martin by the shoulder.

"Surely it is not already morning," said Bertrande.

"No, my dear, it is réveillon. I have brought you your little midnight feast."

"Oh," said Bertrande, "they forgot to tell me about it."

She sat up, looking a little dazed and worried. Without instruction she might not know what to do, she might do the wrong thing. Martin, roused, also sat up, and together they surveyed the tray.

"It is not a bad idea at all," said Martin, his voice foggy with sleep, and, strangely enough, perfectly good-natured.

"Eat," said the woman, beaming upon them. "You have had all the rest of the affair—you may as well enjoy now your little feast, just the two of you. I prepared it myself."

Thus urged, the children rubbed their eyes and fell to, while the woman stood by, her hands on her well-draped hips.

"It is all kinds of an affair, this getting married," she said as she watched the children. "Don't overlook the custard—it is my specialty. And by and by you will appreciate all that your parents have done for you. And meanwhile what peace there is and what friendship in the village of Artigues! You are a pretty little girl, Madame, a little thin, perhaps, but with the years the limbs grow rounder. A little more flesh and you will be altogether charming. And you have a fine, bright color in your cheeks. Look at her, Martin. She is even prettier now than she was at the church, when she was so pale with emotion."

Bertrande ate gravely, licking the yellow custard from the large silver spoon. This was more attention than she had received all day, and, moreover, it was the sort of attention that she could understand. The woman continued in a rich, comfortable voice:

"Take Martin now. He will not be a pretty man, but he will be very distinguished, like his father. There is a kind of ugliness which is very fine in a man. For the rest, I doubt not but that he will be capable of all that is required of a man."

She smiled upon them with no intention of hurrying them, and continued:

"Also, Martin, look at your wife—she has the lucky

eyes, the two-colored eyes, brown and green, and the lucky people bring luck to those they love."

They finished everything upon the tray, even dividing amicably the last bit of pastry between them, and the servant departed with a final word of commendation. Madame Martin Guerre, born Bertrande de Rols, comforted by the inward presence of pastry and custard and by the wholesome unconcern of her husband, fell into a deep untroubled slumber. In the morning she returned to the house of her parents, there to await an age when she should be more fitted to assume her married responsibilities.

So began for the wife of Martin Guerre the estate which was to bring her so much joy and also such strange and unpredictable suffering.

For the present, life went on as usual. She had not gained in personal importance or in liberty by becoming the wife of Martin Guerre; indeed she had not expected to do so. Advantages there were, certainly, from the marriage, but for the present they were all for the two families of Guerre and de Rols; later, Martin and Bertrande would profit from the increased dual prosperity. The solemn ceremony in the church, the recollection of awakening at night to be served royally with delicacies shining on the family plate of les Guerre, receded, overshadowed by the multiplicity of the daily tasks that were her education.

The union of the house of de Rols and that of Guerre had long been considered. It had appeared to three generations as almost inevitable, so many were the advantages for both families to be expected from such an alliance. Three generations ago the matter had been practically settled, until a remark by the great-grandfather of Bertrande de Rols upset the plans of the great-grandfather of Martin Guerre.

"I have a nice little granddaughter whom I'm keeping for you," said the ancestor of Martin to old de Rols, affably, at the close of a conversation which had covered the extent of the mutual benefits which might result from a union between the two families.

"If you wish to keep her well," said the great-grandfather of Bertrande, humorously, "if you wish to keep her very well, my friend, you have only to salt her."

The great-grandfather of Martin regarded de Rols for a moment without speaking, but he was no longer affable.

"You wish to imply then, that she will be easy to keep. You imply that the suitors will not be many. You imply that I may salt her and cover her with oil, like the carcase of a chicken, and she well keep, eh, she will keep indefinitely!"

"My friend, I imply nothing of the sort," said the other old man, patiently. "I only like to have my little joke."

"Your joke," replied Martin's great-grandfather, "your joke is an insult." And he spat in the face of Bertrande de Rols' ancestor.

The negotiations for the marriage were discontinued, and not only that, but great-grandfather Guerre and all his mesnie, that is to say, his sons and daughters and their families, his uncles and aunts and their families, and all the servants whose families had been accustomed to serve these families of the house of Guerre, conceived and maintained an intense hatred of the mesnie of the house of de Rols, which was continued until the birth of Bertrande. Then, since the house of Guerre had rejoiced in the birth of a son but a short time previous, it occurred to the descendants of the jesting and offended great-grandfathers that the best and only way to end a feud of such long standing was to affiance the infants in their cradles. This was accordingly done, and peace was restored.

One should not judge too harshly the pride of the grandfather who was insulted by so mild a jest. As head of his family, the *cap d'hostal,* he carried great responsibilities; the safety and prosperity of all his household depended largely upon the strict obedience and reverence which he could demand from his children, his wife and his servants. From great responsibility arose great pride. No one questioned his right to be offended and no one hesitated to follow his example in hating the offender—offenders, one should say, because the deed of one man became immediately the deed of his family. It is perhaps surprising, however, that the feudal structure should have been maintained so strictly and upon so large a scale by these peasants of Artigues, for these peasants were closer to the *seigneur campagnard* whom the close of the sixteenth century saw coming into prominence than they were to the average peasant of the lowlands, whose families were sprung from the emancipated serfs of the middle ages. The crags and valleys of the Pyrenees were the cause of their prosperity and of their pride.

The hot mineral baths in the valley of Luchon, it is true, were on one of the direct routes from Spain into France, and it is said that the soldiers of Caesar stopped there to soak their battle-weary limbs in the muddy sulphur pools, but the court of Navarre neglected Luchon. The Marguerite of Princesses took her entourage to Cauterets, nearer Pau. Neither was Artigues upon the direct way through the valley of Luchon to the valley of the Garonne. It stood nearer to a small tributary to the Neste in a higher fold of the mountains. It was on the way to no other village. No one visited Artigues who had not business there. And so from generation to generation, while the lowland villages were plundered and burned and their fields laid waste by the religious wars which swept southern France through the thirteenth century and down to the middle of the sixteenth, Artigues enjoyed its isolation and its lack of fame, and actual gold accumulated in the coffers of its more prosperous families. The feudal feeling maintained its value also, as strong as in the earlier centuries, although Francis the First had been for twenty-one years upon the throne of France and although Languedoc had belonged to the French crown almost three hundred years.

When she was fourteen years of age, perhaps a little earlier than might have been the case had it not been for the death of her own mother, Bertrande de Rols went to live finally with the house of Guerre. One deceptively warm autumn forenoon, attended by the servant who had brought the réveillon to the young bridal couple, she crossed the courtyard, barefoot, dressed quite simply in her usual workaday clothes, and found herself on the threshold of the big kitchen. Her mother-in-law kissed her on both cheeks, and led her to the hearth. The wooden coffers which contained her personal effects and the linen and silver of her dowry were carried in and set against the wall, her mother-in-law indicated to her the large bed with the curtains of yellow serge which was to be hers and Martin's, and, without too great haste, she was set to grinding meal in a big stone mortar. Martin and his father were in the fields. Her own father had ridden off to oversee the vintaging. None of the field-workers returned until nightfall. But meanwhile she had time to become familiar with the kitchen, with Martin's four sisters and the servants, with the dogs and cats and with the feathered inhabitants of the basse-cour. She had not visited the house since the day of her wedding, but the scene was much as she had remembered it. The big table on trestles had been removed; there remained only a square table near the hearth, for the family, and a long one beside it for the workers. The floor was strewn only with dried grass, and the walls were not garnished with evergreen; but festoons of garlic and onions, the long stems braided together, hung from the rafters, together with bunches of dried elder blossoms and linden flowers. Bunches of dried rosemary, mountain thyme, and parsley were there also; and, in the hood of the chimney, meats and sausages were freshly hung to benefit from the resinous smoke.

Not again for a long time did Bertrande enjoy as much of her mother-in-law's attention as she did that afternoon, but the leisured kindness and interest which Madame Guerre bestowed upon her son's young wife threw a long warm shadow which extended forward for many days. She showed Bertrande the farm in detail, the stables, the granary, low stone buildings roofed with tile, like the house, set to the right and left of the courtyard before the house; showed her the room used for the dairy, the storerooms with their pots of honey and baskets of fruit, baskets of chestnuts, stone crocks of goose and chicken preserved in oil, eggs buried in bran, cheeses of goat's milk and of cow's milk, wine, oil. In the Chamber she showed her wool and flax for the distaff, the loom on which the clothing for the household would be woven. She showed her the garden, now being set in order for the early frost, the straw-thatched beehives, the sheepfold of mud and wattles, and last of all, returning to the Chamber in which the marriage bed had been dressed, Madame Guerre opened certain chests filled with bran and showed the young girl the coats of mail of the ancestors, thus preserved from rust. She did all this, as Bertrande well knew, that the young wife might understand the household which she would one day be called upon to direct. At no season of the year could she have summarized more happily all that the labors of the spring and summer were working to achieve.

The dusk came early with a chill that presaged winter. It was fully dark before the men began to assemble from the fields and pastures. The tables were set, and fresh bundles of vine trimmings were flung on the fire. The cattle were driven home and stabled, as was necessary every night in the year because of the depredations of bears. The sheep came next, their voices filling the courtyard with a high prolonged babble. The shepherd and the cowherd, entering the kitchen, brought the smell of the beasts into the room. The swineherd came next, and the men who were, turn and turn about, waggoners, vine dressers, or harvesters of grain. Last of all came the head of the family, Martin's father, squired by his son. His wife met him on the threshold with a cup of warmed wine, which he drank before he entered the house. He removed his cape and gave it to one of his daughters. He seated himself at the head of the table. The eldest daughter brought him a bowl of water and a napkin. He washed and wiped his hands, and then, searching the room with his eyes, found Martin's wife and signaled her to approach.

"Sit here, my daughter," he said, indicating a place beside him. "Tonight you shall be waited on. Tomorrow you shall have your own share of the labors of the house."

He did not smile, but the deed and the voice were kind. Bertrande, gazing cautiously into his face as his attention was directed elsewhere, now to the conversation of the shepherd, now toward the blazing hearth, remembered the severe paternal countenance as she had seen it by torchlight from the high pillow of the marriage bed, and she thought that the torchlight had changed it. Here, in the more even glow of the fire, the face of her new father held nothing terrifying. Seamed, coarsened by exposure to rough weather, the darkened skin caught the gold reflections squarely, without compromise or evasion, admitting all the engravures of time. The beard was short, rough and grizzled, parted to show a cleft in the long chin. The mouth, not smiling, but just, had a heavy lower lip which could admit of anger. The nose was short and flattened, the cheek bones were high, the forehead was high and wide, the eyes, now gray, now black, as the light changed, were calmly interested, calm in the assurance of authority. He sat at ease in the stiff-backed rush-bottomed chair, his dark jerkin laced to the throat, his right hand resting on the edge of the table, vigilantly surveying his household, like some Homeric king, some ruler of an island commonwealth who could both plow and fight, and the hand which rested on the table was scarred as from some defensive struggle in years long gone by. Without bearing any outward symbol of his power, he was in his own person both authority and security. He ruled, as the contemporary records say, using the verb which belongs to royalty, and the young girl seated beside him, in feeling this, felt also the great peace which his authority created for his household. It was the first of many evenings in which his presence should testify for her that the beasts were safe, that the grain was safe, that neither the wolves, whose voices could be heard on winter nights, nor marauding bands of mercenaries such as the current hearsay from the larger valleys sometimes reported, could do anything to harm the hearth beside which this man was seated. Because of him the farm was safe, and therefore Artigues, and therefore Languedoc, and therefore France, and therefore the whole world was safe and as it should be.

Martin was sufficiently kind to her, in spite of her apprehensions. He treated her with rather more affection than he did his sisters, bullying her occasionally, as he never bullied them, leaving her for the most part to her own affairs. At night they slept together in their own bed, shoulders turned away from each other, the tired young heads buried deep in the feather-stuffed pillows. Bertrande continued, day by day, her long apprenticeship for the position which she was destined to fill, that of mistress of the farm.

A year went by, during which Bertrande was aware of no other sentiment for her husband than a mild gratitude for his leaving her alone. Then, in the early autumn, Martin went bear-hunting. A cordon had been organized in the parish, according to custom, in order to check to some extent the increasing boldness of those animals which not only destroyed the young barley in the spring but also attacked cattle and sheep. It was generally maintained that there were two species of bear in the Pyrenees, those which were vegetarians strictly and those which were carnivorous. The latter were a far greater menace than the wolves, which were not seen in summer and which were dangerous only in the winter months when stock was likely to be safe in stable or fold. Martin had heard of the cordon, and, without saying anything to anyone, had risen early and gone off to join the hunters. He was not seen all that day. When evening came, the workers returned to the farm, shepherd, swineherd, carter, vintager, but no Martin. Monsieur Guerre inquired for his son, but no one had any information to offer. According to custom, the farm workers and the household servants sat down with their master while Madame Guerre and Bertrande waited upon them. The usual talk of the day's work went on, the meal was finished, the tables were cleared away, and the hour for prayers drew near, before the door burst open and Martin entered, staggering under a load of bearmeat done up in the yet bloody hide of the bear. He was exultant. But when he saw his father's expectant eyes, his exuberance died away, and, depositing his booty before his father, he made his excuses for being absent from the farm labor, and recounted, more briefly than he had intended, the adventures of his day. His father watched him quietly. When the boy had finished, his father said,

"That is all you have to say?"

"Yes, my father."

"Very well. Kneel."

Martin dropped on his knees, and his father, leaning forward, struck him with the knuckles of his right hand full upon the left side of his jaw. Martin said nothing. Madame Guerre caught her breath but made no outcry. In a moment Martin stood up and went to spit blood into the fire.

"Prayers, my children," said the father.

The household, upon its knees, with bowed heads, attended to the prayers which the father repeated, and then, dispersing, went off to bed. Several hours later that evening when the house was quiet and only a small gleam of firelight shone through the folds of serge which enclosed their bed, Bertrande said to Martin:

"Are you awake?"

"Certainly. My jaw aches. He has broken me two teeth."

"It was not just," she whispered with indignation.

"Certainly it was just. I didn't ask him if I might go. I was afraid that he might refuse me. But it was well done, was it not, to kill a bear?"

"Oh, yes," she replied fervently. "Martin, you are brave."

He said nothing to that, agreeing in his heart, but as he fell asleep, later, his arm rested on her shoulder. She had sided with him against the paternal authority, however just that authority might be. They were two, a camp within a camp. As for Bertrande, to her own surprise she began to understand that Martin belonged to her and that her affection for him was even greater than her respect and admiration for his father.

In the morning Madame Guerre, examining the damage done to her son's teeth, wept, but did not protest against her husband's severity.

"You understand, my son, it is necessary," she said. "If you have no obedience for your father, your son will have none for you, and then what will become of the family? Ruin. Despair."

"Yes, my mother, I understand," said Martin.

No one but Bertrande had hinted that the punishment was arbitrary and severe, and nothing further was said by anyone about the matter.

But gradually Bertrande's affection for her husband became a deep and joyous passion, growing slowly and naturally as her body grew. All about her, life flourished and increased itself, in field, in fold, in the rose-flushed bramble stems of spring before the green leaf unfurled, and in the vine leaves of autumn that lay like fire along the corded branches. She felt this passion within herself like the wine they drank in the early days of spring, light, tart, heady, and having a special fragrance, and her delight illuminated her love like the May sunshine pouring downward into the cupped wine. Early in her twentieth year she gave birth to a son, and her happiness seemed crowned and sanctified beyond anything she had ever dreamed. They called the boy Sanxi. His grandfather, receiving him in his arms a few minutes after his birth, rubbed his lips with garlic and touched them with a few sour drops of the wine of the country, welcoming him as a true Gascon. The boy thrived, and his mother thrived with him, as if they lent each other well-being.

Being the mother of an heir, Bertrande now received from her parents-in-law a new esteem which was manifest in little favors. This filled her with pride and contributed in no small measure to the grace with which she carried her dark head. More than ever she understood her position in the household, part of a structure that reached backward in time towards ancestors of whose renown one was proud and forward to a future in which Sanxi was a young man, in which Sanxi's children were to grow tall and maintain, as she and Martin now helped to maintain, the prosperity and honor of the family.

Martin had been placed in full charge of certain labors of the farm, and more especially in charge of certain fields. He was responsible to his father for all he did, but the method and the details were in his own hands. It was a part of his progress toward the assumption of the full authority of the farm, which could not come to him until after his father's death, but for which he must be early prepared.

His situation was moreover curious in this respect; for the extent of his father's lifetime Martin would remain legally a minor. He might grow old, Sanxi might marry and have sons, but as long as the elder Guerre survived, so long was he absolute head of the house, and such liberty as Martin might enjoy was to be enjoyed only under his father's rule. This was so well understood together with the necessity for the law, that it never occurred to Martin to suppose it might be otherwise. It was known throughout Languedoc that a father owned the privilege of freeing his son, if he chose, from the parental authority, but this could only be done through a deliberate and formal ceremony; and although there were fathers who sometimes so liberated their sons, if anyone had asked Martin

Guerre what he thought of such a procedure, he would almost certainly have replied that he thought ill. All such authority as belonged to the *cap d'hostal* Martin Guerre wished to retain, however much he might personally suffer for the time being under such authority. After the lapse of years he expected himself to be *cap d'hostal,* and when that responsibility should rest upon him he would have need of all the accumulated authority of antiquity, even as his father had need of it now.

Martin resembled his father greatly, both physically and in disposition. Bertrande, who sometimes observed his smothered resentment, or impatience at his inferior position, understood both the impatience and the attitude which kept it in control, the acceptance of things as they were, and said quietly to herself:

"In his day he will make a protector for this family as like his own father as two men well may be, and for that thanks to God."

Outwardly, Martin had the swarthy skin, the high forehead, the gray eyes, the flat, short nose, the lips, the high cleft chin of his father, and something of his father's build. Too early labor at the plow had rounded his shoulders. Nevertheless he was a skillful swordsman and boxer, agile, tall, and well-developed for his years. "Not a pretty man," as the servant had said, "but a very distinguished man." His ugliness was ancestral, and that in itself was good.

People so reasonable, so devoted, so strongly loving and hard working should have been exempt, one feels, from the vagaries of a malicious fate. Nevertheless, the very virtues of their way of life gave rise to a small incident, and from that incident developed the whole train of misfortune which singled out Bertrande de Rols from the peace and obscurity of her tradition.

It was a day in autumn. The vintage was done and the winter wheat was being put in the ground. Since the men were not expected to return to the farm at noon, Bertrande had taken Martin's lunch to him, and while he ate, she sat beside him on the sun-warmed, roughened earth at the edge of the field. She was bare-footed and bare-headed, the bodice of her gown open a little at the throat because of the noonday heat. The flesh at the edge of the gown was creamy, and the color deepened upward into a warm tan, growing richer and brighter on the rounded cheeks; and at the edge of the hair, in the shadow of the thick dark locks, the creamy color showed again, now moist from the sheltered heat. She watched her husband with tender, happy eyes. Before them, the cultivated ground slanted downward to a hazel copse. They could hear above them the murmur of the stream, reduced from its full summer flow, where it ran under the chestnut trees, before it circled the field, running below them through the copse and on into the narrowing valley. Across the valley and on the higher slopes, the beech and oak woods were tinged with gold and russet, and higher still a blue haze seemed to be gathering, like threads of smoke. Leaf, earth, and wine in the still sunlight gave forth the odors of their substances; the air was full of autumn fragrance. Martin, when he had finished his lunch, wrapped the fragments of bread and cheese and put them in his wallet. He returned the earthen wine jug to the hands of his wife and said:

"I am going away for a little while."

Bertrande made an exclamation of surprise.

"You may well be astonished," replied Martin. "This is the way of it. This morning I took from my father's granary enough seed wheat to plant the half of this field."

"You did not ask him for it?" cried Bertrande in alarm.

"Certainly, no. He would have denied it to me because it is his notion that I should put aside whatever grain I need from my own harvesting. But this year I have more land under cultivation than I had hoped to have. Should I let it go to waste? He has finished his planting; the wheat remains unused. So I took it, and I have planted it. Was it not well done?"

"It was well done," she answered, "but I am afraid for you."

"I am afraid for myself," he said with a smile. "Without a doubt, he would flay me. Therefore I am going away. When he has had time to reflect, he will see that it was well done, and he will forgive me. Then I can return. You remember the bear?"

He rubbed his hand reminiscently along his jaw while Bertrande also smiled a little.

"You will have to be gone at least a week," she said. "Perhaps longer. If I could send you word . . ."

"Eight days should be enough," said Martin. "It is done for the good of the house—he will see that. And it is better that you should not know where I am in case he asks you. I shall go to Toulouse, then further, so that you can answer honestly, 'I do not know where he is.' Embrace my little son for me, and do not be disturbed."

She kissed him on both cheeks, feeling the warmth of the sun upon his flesh, caressing with her hand the short smooth beard, and then, in a brief premonition of disaster, held to his arm and would not let him go.

"Do not distress yourself," he repeated tenderly. "I shall be safe. I shall enjoy myself, moreover. And I shall see you in a week."

So he went off. Once he turned to wave with a free, elated gesture, and then the shadows of the trees engulfed his figure. Bertrande returned to the farm, swinging the empty jug from a forefinger and thinking of the path which led down the valley beside the torrent falling and tumbling toward the Neste. Once she stepped aside to let pass a herd of swine being driven up into the oak forest to feed on acorns. She greeted the swineherd absently, thinking of Martin's journey, and how he would pass village after village, ford the cold streams, follow the narrow passes beside the Neste and eventually emerge into the greater valley of the Garonne, see the level fields, the walled cities, broad roads traversed by bands of merchants and armed men. The woods were still after the passage of the beasts—no insects and few birds. She wished that she might have gone with Martin. At the farm she found Sanxi, and was glad that she had not gone.

The afternoon passed as usual, but at suppertime, when Monsieur Guerre asked her where Martin was, and she answered, as had been arranged between them, "I do not know," she trembled beneath the cold gray gaze, penetrating and clear as a beam of light reflected from a wall of ice.

When it was learned that certain baskets of grain had been removed from the granary, the anger of Monsieur Guerre was terrible, as she had known it would be, and she was thankful that Martin's shoulders were beyond the reach of his father's heavy whip. At the end of a week the anger of Monsieur Guerre had not abated. Apprehensively Bertrande listened at the approach of every passer-by, started and turned cold each time the door to the house creaked on its broad hinges, and hoped that Martin might be fortunately delayed. Again and again she wished that some arrangement had been made between them by which she might meet and warn him. As week followed week, alarm at his prolonged absence began to mingle with the fear of his premature return. At the end of a month she was almost certain that some evil must have befallen him, and in great fear and agitation presented herself before the father of the family and confessed all that she knew of Martin's design.

Monsieur Guerre listened to her in silence, without moving a finger. Then he answered coldly:

"Madame, that my son should have become a thief is the greatest shame I have ever been asked to bear. Since he is my son, my only son, and since the welfare of the house depends upon the succession of an heir, I consider it my duty to forgive him. When he returns and confesses his crime, and has borne his punishment, I shall withdraw my anger. Until that time, no matter how distant it may be, rest assured, Madame, my anger shall exist. You may return to your work, Madame."

It was terrible to her to be addressed in this manner by a man whom she so greatly respected. "For their children," wrote the learned Etienne Pasquier a few years later, "fathers and mothers are the true images of God upon earth," and this was not an opinion which Pasquier imposed upon his time, but one in which he had been schooled. Bertrande admitted the inflexible justice of Martin's father, and regretted bitterly that she had fallen in with Martin's plans for avoiding punishment. How much better if he had stayed and submitted! He would now be forgiven and all would be well. She now prayed that he return at once. But the winter deepened about the village of Artigues, the ways were blocked with snow, and as even the mountain torrent became locked under ice she abandoned all hope of seeing him that winter.

It was lonely without him. The days, shortened by the double shadow of winter and of the steep mountain-sides, held little gaiety for the wife of Martin Guerre, and the nights were unutterably long. When spring came, the snow melted and all the valley was murmurous with the sound of rushing water. Still Martin delayed his return, and she said to herself:

"It is too early to hope for him. All the streams are flooded, the fords are impassable. Men and horses have been drowned trying to cross La Neste in flood."

She said this, but still her heart unreasonably demanded that he return and that quickly. With the first fine weather, the young wheat sprouting, the vines beginning to put forth tufts of silvery, crumpled leaves, with the half-wooded, half-cultivated valley ringing, now far, now near, with birdsong, her own youth and beauty quickened; and together with her consciousness of her youth, her beauty, her desire deepened for her husband. Somehow, with the winter, had died the fear that Martin might have been hurt or killed. She was at that time too young to believe in the reality of death. The reviving season held only her love and her impatience.

But spring went by, and Martin did not return. Through the deepening summer she looked for him in vain and only when the first heavy snow again closed the mountain passes did she admit to herself that her husband had left her. She knew that he had found the experience of liberty sweet, that to be master of his own actions was more precious to him than the society of his wife, the enjoyment of his son, or his share in the prosperity of the house. She believed that Martin was waiting until the time when he might return as head of the house, that he could not brook the idea of returning, not only to punishment, but to the continued rigors of his father's authority. She said nothing of this to anyone, but the thought was not an easy one to live with.

He had deserted her in the full beauty of her youth, in the height of her great passion, he had shamed her and wounded her, and when he returned, if he should return after the death of his father, his authority would be as great as his father's then was, and to murmur against his treatment of her would then be improper in the highest degree.

Martin's absence weighed upon the whole family. Although his father never mentioned his name, it was evident to those who knew him well that he had aged since Martin's departure. The second year after the disappearance of her son, Madame Guerre died. She was not an old woman, and it may have been possible, as her daughters believed, that the illness from which she suffered during the last year of her life was greatly aggravated by the prolonged absence of her son. Bertrande assumed her duties and mourned her, for whatever their differences, always unexpressed by Bertrande, on other matters, the deserted wife had felt that her mother-in-law retained no anger against Martin. With Monsieur Guerre it was quite another matter. However perfect his courtesy to her, Bertrande felt always in his presence the just, inflexible displeasure that he maintained toward her husband, and she was reminded, also, that she had shared in Martin's plan. To his original offense, as time went by, Martin was also adding the greater offense of neglecting his inheritance.

The displeasure of Monsieur Guerre had become as necessary and inevitable a part of his character as his spine was of his body. When he entered a room that displeasure entered with him. The household, meanwhile, had changed and was no longer gay. Martin's elder sisters had married and lived elsewhere. The youngest, having married a cadet, or younger son, still lived at home and her husband had come to live with her. He was a quiet soul, deferring easily to Bertrande and to Monsieur Guerre. His presence did not greatly enliven the scene. Sanxi, who was excessively healthy, did not know how to be unhappy, and whether he played or rested, the place where he happened to be was for his mother the only joyous spot on the farm. For the rest, the household waited. Work went on, but the feeling of expectation was always in the air.

The fourth year after Martin's departure his father, though an expert horseman, was thrown from his horse, and, his head striking against a rock as he fell, he was killed instantly. Bertrande, who had seen him ride away from the house, firm and erect in the saddle, could hardly believe the servants who came with the news an hour later. Still, there was something fitting in the manner of his death, which was abrupt, violent and absolute. The peremptory summons and the prompt obedience were like everything else in his way of living. It would have been difficult to conceive of him as grown old, yielding, little by little, perforce, his authority, hesitating and dwindling, and yet, if Martin had not returned, holding on to a life thoroughly exhausted in order not to leave the house without a master.

The shock of his death threw the family into confusion. Something like a panic seemed to overpower the servants and to reduce the four sisters of Martin to helpless children. And yet at the end of the day, Bertrande, finding for the first time a moment to herself, was surprised to consider how completely his death had been accepted, how long he seemed to have been dead who was not yet buried, whose death, early that morning, has been almost as remote as the day of judgment.

Pierre Guerre, the brother of Monsieur Guerre, had arrived in the afternoon and had announced his position as head of the family. He was a lesser man than his brother, shorter and broader of frame, with something of the family countenance but without the quality of great distinction that somehow had belonged to the old master. No less honest, but more simple, easier to approach, a good farmer, a solid soldier, Uncle Pierre had entered the kitchen and crossed with sober dignity to his brother's chair by the hearth. He had assigned tasks, taken the legal matters into consideration, sent for the priest and made public the news of the death. The panic had subsided, the servants had gone about their business as usual, the older sisters had returned to their homes, and Bertrande had said to herself:

"Now it will be safe for Martin to return."

She did not expect him to appear magically. She made her own estimate of the time that it might take the news, traveling uncertainly about the countryside, to reach him, and how long it would take him to make the journey home. And hope flourished and wore greener branches than in many a long day. But as the year which she had allowed passed on and drew to a close, her hope again declined, and there were times when despair took its place entirely. She no longer had the fine sense of immortality which she had felt before the death of Martin's parents. Death had now become an actuality rather than a possibility. Death was something that not only could happen but that did happen.

A new fear assailed her. When she thought of Martin as perhaps dead, his remembered features suddenly dissolved, and the more she strove to recollect his appearance, the vaguer grew her memory. When she was not trying to remember him, his face would sometimes reappear, suddenly distinct in color and outline. Then she would start and tremble inwardly and try to hold the vision. But the harder she tried, the dimmer grew the face. The same thing had happened to her, she now remembered, after her mother's death. The beloved image had faded. An impression of warmth, of security, the tones of the voice, the pressure of the hand had remained, but she could not see her mother's face. She had spoken of this to Madame Guerre, who had replied:

"There are people like that. They do not remember

with their eyes, but with their ears, maybe. With me, it is the eye, and I could tell you at any moment in which chest I have laid away anything that you might want. I do not remember where it is, I see it. I cast my eye, as it were, over all my arrangements, and I see where I have laid the article which you desire."

Once indeed Bertrande thought that Martin had returned. She was walking on the path to the lower fields and was near the place where she had said farewell to her husband almost five years before. A man coming toward her under the shadow of the trees moved with Martin's gait and was so like him in build that Bertrande stopped, her hand on her breast and her heart leaping suddenly in such wild delight that she could hardly breathe. But the figure, approaching, lost its likeness to the man she loved. She saw presently that he was a stranger and that his features did not resemble those of Martin Guerre in the least. He did not even come near enough to pass her, but some few yards away turned off into the woods in the direction of Sode. Their eyes had met, like those of strangers who met in a narrow path, and he had saluted her, but without recognition.

After he had gone, she stood there, ready to weep in her sick disappointment. The day was cool, a day toward the end of winter, and she wore a heavy black wool cape with a hood, and on her feet were the pointed wooden sabots of her mountains, but she seemed to be standing barefoot on the moss, and bareheaded. Martin's hands were upon hers; she could see the familiar scars, the torn fingernail; and Martin's head was bent and touching hers. She could not see his face for his cheek was against her forehead.

From the pressure of his hands upon hers such peace and joy flowed into her body that all the woods seemed warm, bathed in autumnal sunlight. The moment faded and she stood alone again in the thin winter air. She realized then that she had not seen his face, and wondered if that might be of good or bad omen. But the touch of his hand had been very living, and she renewed her hope.

If she heard of there being strangers in town, as there so often were, smugglers from Spain, or deserters from one army for another passing from kingdom to kingdom by way of the Port de la Venasque who delayed their wanderings to visit awhile in the rich mountain villages, she sent for them and entertained them overnight, giving them food, wine and a warm place to sleep. Of these she inquired for news of Martin. Had they, while serving with the Duke of Savoy or under the old Constable Montmorency or with the young Duke of Guise, heard of any man named Martin Guerre? Or bivouacked with him? Or perhaps fought by his side? None of these wanderers had met with such a man. They gave her, in return for her hospitality, other news, of how, before the death of the old king, Guienne, Angoumois and Saintonge had risen in insurrection because of the salt tax, of how at Angoulême the king's tax collectors had been beaten to death and sent "to salt the fish of the Charente," their flesh being flung into the river. She heard of the cruel revenge which Montmorency took under the new king, Henry, the second of that name, at Bordeaux, burning alive those who had killed the tax collectors, and oppressing and humiliating the whole city most grievously. She learned of the siege of Metz and of Henry's continuance of the quarrels of his father with the Emperor from men who had fought with Guise under the walls of that city. The Emperor had said, "I see now that Fortune is a woman; she prefers a young king to an old emperor," and, fatigued and ill, "his face all pale and his eyes sunk in his head, his beard as white as the snow," had made his resolve to abdicate and withdraw to Yuste, there on the other side of the Pyrenees in the Spanish monastery of the Cordeliers. Her imagination traveled far afield, thinking that wherever there was fighting, there Martin was likely to be; but of Martin himself she learned nothing. She charged these wanderers, upon their leave-taking, with a message to her husband, if they should chance to meet him:

"The old Master is dead. Come home."

She even made a journey once to Rieux, where her mother's sister then lived, thinking that to that town, which was a bishopric, almost as many travelers must come as to Toulouse. The town lay in a green meadow in a curve of the Arize, near to the spot at which that turbulent stream hurls itself into the Garonne. Behind it stood the wall of the Pyrenees. The delicate, bold spire of the cathedral, rising above the tiled roofs of the houses, seemed less tall than it was because of the height of the mountains. At the inn and at the cathedral doors Bertrande made her inquiries, and besought her aunt to question travelers whenever she might have the opportunity. She also begged that the death of Martin's father be announced from the cathedral. But a nostalgia came upon her there—she had never before left the parish of Artigues. She missed Sanxi, and everything seemed strange. Even the room in which she slept in her aunt's house seemed turned around, and the sun rose in the west and shone through western windows all the morning. Or so it seemed to Bertrande. After a few days she made her excuses to her aunt, and went home to Artigues.

And time went by. Meanwhile Sanxi, who in his earliest infancy had given some slight promise of growing to look like his father, daily grew more and more to resemble the sisters of Martin Guerre, who had their mother's features and proportions rather than those of their father. This was at first a grief to Bertrande, although in considering Sanxi with his fresh young face and thick smooth chestnut hair, he seemed to her so altogether remarkable and charming that she could not wish him otherwise in any detail. She began to listen instead for the tones of his father's voice in the boy's light treble. So, nourishing her devotion with hope and with imagination, she took charge of Martin's household, tended his child, and waited.

The house flourished, Sanxi grew, and Bertrande increased in beauty. Her sorrow and her new sense of responsibility ennobled her physical charm. She acquired unconsciously a manner of gracious command. Eight years after the departure of her husband she no longer had the first tender radiance which had so pleased the young man, but a greater and more mature beauty had taken its place.

Eight years after the departure of Martin Guerre, Bertrande his wife was seated in the Chamber instructing her son in the catechism. The first warm days of summer were come, and neither mother nor son was paying as great attention as might have been paid to the lesson in hand. The room, large, dusky, cool, shut them effectively from the affairs of the kitchen and the courtyard. The wooden shutters were opened wide, but the window was high. It let in the sunshine but did not permit a view of the yard. The peace of the summer day without, the quiet half hour alone with Sanxi, the release from the continual round of practical duties had relaxed Bertrande. She looked at Sanxi's cool young cheek beside her knee and thought, "At last I begin to be at peace."

And her thought, sweeping backward quickly over all the moments of anguish, of desire, of hatred, even, hours of fierce resentment against Martin for making her suffer, for holding her from any other life than a prolonged fruitless waiting for his return, hours of terror when she had contemplated his death in some engagement of the Spanish wars, hours to be remembered with horror in which she had desired his death that she might be free of the agony of incertitude—all these reviewed in a moment with a sharp inward knowledge of herself, her thought returned like a tired dove to this moment of peace in which love was only love for Sanxi, as innocent and cool and gentle as the curve of his cheek. She regarded him thoughtfully and tenderly, and Sanxi, lifting his eyes to hers, smiled with a secret amusement.

"Repeat the answer, my son," said Bertrande.

Sanxi did so, his delight deepening.

"But you have given me that reply for two questions, Sanxi. You do not attend."

"No, mother, for three questions, the same answer," said Sanxi, suddenly hilarious.

"You must not make fun of sacred things," she said to him as gravely as she could, but neither of them was deceived, and as they smiled at each other, a hubbub arose in the courtyard which made Sanxi run to the window. Standing on his tiptoes, he still could not see much but the adjoining buildings. The tumult increased, with shrill cries, definitely joyous. Bertrande de Rols turned toward the door, leaning slightly forward in her chair. The noise, advancing through the kitchen, was approaching the Chamber, and suddenly the door swung open to admit Martin's Uncle Pierre, his four sisters and a bearded man dressed in leather and steel, who paused on the threshold as the others crowded forward. Behind him all the household servants and one or two men from the fields showed their excited ruddy faces. The old housekeeper, pushing past him, almost beside herself with joy, curtsied as low as she could, and cried:

"It is he, Madame!"

"It is Martin, my child," said Uncle Pierre.

"Bertrande," cried the sisters in chorus, "here is our brother Martin!"

Their voices filled the room, echoing from the low beams and the stone walls; they were all talking at once, and, as Bertrande rose to her feet, keeping one hand on the back of the chair to steady herself against a sudden, quickly passing dizziness, the bearded figure advanced gravely, surrounded by the agitated forms of the sisters, the uncle, the servants, who were now all swarming in behind the original group.

It was dark at the far end of the room. Bertrande stood in the sunlight and met, as in a dream, the long-anticipated moment, her breath stilled and her heart beating wildly. The figure in leather and steel advanced with even tread, a stockier figure than that of the man who had gone away eight years before, broader in the shoulder, developed, mature. The beard was strange, being rough and thick, but above it the eyes were like those of Martin, the forehead, the whole cast of the countenance, like and unlike to Bertrande's startled recognition, and as he advanced from the shadow he seemed to Bertrande a stranger, the stranger of the wooded pathway, then her loved husband, then a man who might have been Martin's ancestor but not young Martin Guerre.

When he had advanced to within a few feet of her, he stopped, and she read in his eyes a surprise and an admiration so intense that her limbs seemed all at once bathed in a soft fire. She was frightened.

"Madame," said the stranger who was her husband, "you are very beautiful."

"Cap de Diou!" exclaimed the uncle. "Are you surprised that your wife is beautiful?"

"Beautiful, yes, I knew, but beauty such as this I did not remember."

"Yes, Martin, yes," cried the sisters. "She has changed, you are right. It is another beauty."

"But why do you stand there? Embrace her, my nephew."

And then Bertrande felt on her cheek the imprint of the bearded lips, and on her shoulders the weight of the strong hands, felt with a shock the actual masculinity of the embrace, so strange for one who had been long accustomed only to the light touch of Sanxi's mouth. The embrace released her from her trance, reminding her of the last kiss which she had given Martin at the edge of the wheat field, and all the emotion tightly held in check for so many years was in her voice as she cried:

"Ah, why have you been away so long! Cruel! Cruel! I have almost forgotten your face! Even your voice, Martin, is strange in my ears."

"Bertrande," said Pierre Guerre with gravity, "this is no proper welcome for your husband, to overwhelm him with reproaches. You forget yourself, my child, indeed you do. My nephew, you must pardon her. It is the excess of emotion. We cannot tell you how we rejoice at your return. It was the greatest of sorrows to your father that you were gone so long. But that is over. I praise God that you are safely with us, no longer a boy, but a man grown. In times like these a house has need of a master and a child of a protector."

"I praise God also," said Bertrande softly, "and I ask your pardon, my husband."

"No, Uncle," came the reply. "She does well to reproach the man who left you all so long unprotected. It is I who should ask pardon of her. But you must believe me: until I passed through Rieux I did not know that my father was dead." And, bending above her hand, he promised Bertrande that he would never again leave her and that he would do all in his power to atone for the neglect which he had shown her. Bertrande was deeply touched and not a little surprised. Uncle Pierre remarked:

"It is well done, my nephew. I can see that the wars have done more for you than strengthen bone and muscle. You have spoken like a true father and like the head of a house."

Behind him the four sisters of Martin were agitated by murmurs of approval, and there were cries of approval and admiration from the servants, who, crowding forward, all wished to salute their long-absent master.

He greeted them all, inquiring for certain ones who had died during his absence, questioned them about their families and their health, praised them for their loyalty and good service, and appeared so genuinely pleased to see them all that their enthusiasm redoubled.

Bertrande, watching him, said to herself:

"He is noble, he is generous, he is like his father again, but become gracious."

But suddenly the master, putting aside gently the servants who stood between him and Bertrande, cried:

"But where is Sanxi? Where is my son, that I may embrace him?"

At this Sanxi, who had been hiding behind his mother, burrowed his head into her skirts, drawing the ample folds about his shoulders.

"Come, Sanxi," said his mother, taking him by the shoulders. "Here is your father, your good father of whom we have talked so many times. Salute him."

"Ah, my little monsieur," exclaimed a great voice, "it is good to see you," and Sanxi, clinging like a kitten to his mother's skirts, so that she had to disengage his fingers one by one, felt himself hoisted into the air and then folded close to a hard shoulder, smelt the reek of leather and horse-sweat, and then felt the wiry beard rubbed joyously against his face.

"Mama!" he cried. "Mama!"

"It is the strangeness," he heard his mother's voice saying apologetically. "Do not hold it against him. Consider, how sudden and how strange—for him, as for me."

"Tonnèrre!" cried the great voice. "He is hard to hold. But never mind. We shall be friends, in time."

The boy felt himself set on his feet firmly, and then his parents turned away from him. Some people pushed in between him and his mother, and as the crowd moved toward the door, everyone laughing and talking, it carried her along, clinging to the arm of the stranger. The swineherd and the boy who cared for the horses were the last to leave the room. They lagged behind, buffeting each other out of sheer good will, and the swineherd, turning, saw young Sanxi still standing in front of his mother's chair.

"What a fine day for you," he called. "It isn't everyday that a boy gets a father."

An hour later Sanxi had recovered himself sufficiently to dare sit beside his father on the long bench before the fireplace. On the other side of his father was the priest; in front of him, on a stool, was Uncle Pierre. His mother kept coming and going from the table to the fireplace, pausing sometimes with her hand on the shoulder of Uncle Pierre to gaze happily and incredulously at his father.

Uncle Pierre had to tell again how he had met Sanxi's father, "away by the church, far from the road to the farm. I knew him at once, and that from the back of his head. I cried, 'Hollah, Martin, my nephew, where are you going, away so far from your own house? You have returned,' I said. 'Pray do not leave us before you have seen your own roof.' And what answer did he make, this excellent man? 'I am going,' said he, 'to the church to give thanks to God for my safe return and to pray for the soul of my father of whose death I learned only yesterday.' "

The priest nodded with grave approval; the uncle wiped an actual tear from his eye.

"So then I cried, 'Good boy, embrace me, Martin, embrace your old Uncle Pierre,' and together we went and knelt in the church. I am glad that I have lived to see this day."

Then Sanxi's father had to hear from the priest and from Uncle Pierre all the story of how Sanxi's grandfather had fallen from his horse and been killed instantly, and of how his grandmother had died very quietly in her bed with all her family and her servants round about, weeping, all save her son Martin, and through all these recitals Sanxi was puzzled to see how his mother alternately wept and smiled. His father did not cry. He was very serious, very serious and strong, and Sanxi, sitting beside him, observed minutely all the straps and buckles of his armor and how the metal of his gorget had chafed the leather of his jerkin, and began to admire him, silently.

For the rest of the day he attached himself to his father's person, like a small dog who does not mind whether he is noticed or not, provided he is permitted to be present. He heard his father's brief account of his wanderings. He listened to the servants as they poured out to his father their stories of everything that had taken place since his departure, eight years ago. He even listened unnoticed while Uncle Pierre went over the business of the house with his father. And in the evening there were violins and flutes, roast meat as if it were a fête day, and neighbors riding in from miles around to welcome his father home. Sanxi had not known that his own household could be so gay. The very walls of the kitchen were animated and seemed to tremble in the ruddy glow from the chimney. The copper vessels winked and blazed. The glazed pottery on the dresser also gave back the quivering light, and his father's armor, as he flung himself back in his chair, or rose to meet a newcomer, was momentarily like the sky of an autumn sunset.

But the seasons are tyrannical for the farmer. In the morning the flutes and violins were put away, and before dawn the men were about the usual work of the farm. The master to the fields, the mistress to the dairy—everything was just as usual until evening, and then, after supper before the hour for prayers, there was much talk by the fireplace of foreign lands, sieges and marches, the slaying of heretics, and finally, instead of his mother saying, "Prayers, my friends," there was the master of the house, like Sanxi's grandfather, announcing,

"My children, it is time for prayer."

The estate prospered surprisingly after the return of the master. The vigor of the man was contagious, and he had a way of noticing the work that a servant was doing and saying a word of approval that the old master had never had. For Bertrande, as for Sanxi, it was a new life, almost a new world. Gladly she surrendered the responsibilities of the farm to her husband's care, and surrendered herself to his love. From having been a widow for eight years, she was suddenly again a wife. The loneliness of the house was dissipated. Even when there were not old friends come from a distance to greet Martin Guerre, even when the priest was not established in the corner of the hearth to hear accounts of the world below the mountains, there was good conversation in the house, and sometimes music, and Sanxi flourished and grew manly in the companionship of a hero. His newly-found father was no less to him.

At the end of a few months Bertrande found herself with child. She rejoiced thereat, and she also trembled, for at times a curious fear assailed her, a fear so terrible and unnatural that she hardly dared acknowledge it in her most secret heart. What if Martin, the roughly bearded stranger, were not the true Martin, the one whom she had kissed farewell that noonday by the side of the freshly planted field? Her sin, if such indeed were a fact, would be most black, for had she not experienced an instinctive warning? On the night of his return, overcome by desire and astonishment, she had trembled in his embrace and murmured again and again:

"Martin, it is so strange, I cannot believe it to be true."

To which the bearded traveler had replied:

"Poor little one, you have been too long alone."

In the morning her fear had vanished, Martin's family and friends, the servants, the very animals of the place, it seemed, affirming his identity, and putting her heart at peace.

So she had been happy, and had rejoiced in the presence of this new Martin even more than in that of the old, and it was not until she began to feel the weight of the child in her body that the fear returned. Even so, it did not stay. It was like the shadow of a dark wing sweeping suddenly across the room, and then departing swiftly as it had come, leaving all things standing as usual under the cold, normal light of day. But one day, seeing Martin returning from a ride with Sanxi, and seeing the easy comradeship between the two, she said aloud:

"It is not possible that this man should be Martin Guerre. For Martin Guerre, the son of the old master, proud and abrupt, like the old master, could never in this world speak so gaily to his own son. Ah! unhappy woman that I am, so to distrust the Good God who has sent me this happiness! I shall be punished. But this is also punishment in itself."

No one heard her speak, and, weeping bitterly, she withdrew to her own room where she remained until a servant came to find her at the hour of the evening meal. Nevertheless, in spite of her contrition, she could not refrain, the moment that they were left alone that evening, from accusing her husband of being other than the man he represented, and of asking for proof of his identity.

She had expected passionate proof or passionate denial. The man before her regarded her gravely, even tenderly, and said:

"Proof? But why proof? You have seen me. You have felt the touch of my lips. Behold my hands. Are they not scarred even as you remember them? Do you remember the time my father struck me and broke my teeth? They are still broken. You have spoken with me; we have spoken together of things past. Is not my speech the same? Why should I be other than myself? What has happened to give you this strange notion?"

Bertrande replied in a barely audible voice:

"If you had been Martin Guerre you would perhaps have struck me just now."

He answered with gentle surprise:

"But because I struck you on the day we were married, is that a reason I should strike you now? Listen to me, my dearest. Am I who speak to you now more different from the young man who left you, than that young man was different from the child you married?"

"When you left me," said Bertrande, "you resembled your father in flesh and spirit. Now you resemble him only in the flesh."

"My child," said her husband, ever more gravely, "my father was arrogant and severe. Just, also, and loving, but his severity sent from home his only son. For eight years I have traveled among many sorts and conditions of men. I have been many times in danger of death. If I return to you with a greater wisdom than that which I knew when I departed, would you have me dismiss it, in order again to resemble my father? God knows, my child, and the priest will so instruct you, that a man of evil ways may by an act of will so alter all his actions and his habits that he becomes a man of good. Are you satisfied?"

"And then," said Bertrande, in a still smaller voice, marshaling her last argument, "Martin Guerre at twenty had not the gift of the tongue. His father, also, was a silent man."

At this her husband, hitherto so grave, burst into a laugh which made the Chamber echo, and still laughing, with his broad hand he wiped the tears from her wet face.

"My darling, how funny you are," he said. "Weep no more. Every Gascon has the gift of the tongue. Some employ it, some do not. Since I am become no longer arrogant and severe, I choose to employ my gift." Then, more gently, he continued. "Madame, you are demented. It happens sometimes to women who are with child. Pay no attention to it. It will pass, and when your time is over, you will look back to this with astonishment."

"Perhaps that is it," said Bertrande in acquiescence. "For God knows I do not wish you to be otherwise than my true husband. When I went to visit my aunt in Rieux, being in a strange town, I became confused as to the directions, and not until I left that house did it seem to me, when I was within doors, that the east was not the west. So it must be with me now. For when I look at you it seems to me that I see the flesh and bone of Martin Guerre, but in them I see dwelling the spirit of another man."

"When I was in Brittany," said her husband, "I heard a strange story of a man who was also a wolf, and there may also have been times when the soul of one man inhabited the body of another. But it is also notorious that men who have been great sinners have become saints. What would become of us all if we had no power to turn from evil toward good?"

And so he led her on to talk of other matters, of foreign lands and battles in Flanders until she was again calm. She put her fear away, or rather, she regarded it as a delusion, and she gave herself over to the happy anticipation of her second child. In her affection for her husband was now mingled a profound gratitude, for he had delivered her, at least for the present, from the terror of sin. When, upon a certain day she asked him if he remembered such and such a little incident, and he responded, smiling, "No, and do you remember when I told you that your eyes are speckled like the back of a mountain trout?" she only smiled in return, full of confidence and ease.

"You did not say such things when you were twenty," she replied.

It was the time of year when the grapes were being harvested, and the odor of ripe muscats was in the air. When the wine was made and the leaves on the vine stocks had turned scarlet, Bertrande rode out among valleys that dipped in fire toward Luchon between the irregular advances of the woods, saw the conical haystacks burning with dull gold beside the stone walls of farm buildings, felt, as she rode in the sunshine, the cold invigorating sweep of wind from the higher mountains, lifted her eyes and saw how the white clouds piled high above the rich green of the pine woods and how the sky was intensely blue beyond, blue as a dream of the Mediterranean or of the Gulf of Gascony. And returning, toward evening to her own house, as the blue haze of evening began to intercept and transmute the shapes of things, she smelled the wood smoke from her own hearth fire and thought it as sweet as the incense which was burned in the church at Artigues. Or she saw at the far end of a field, a man wearing a scarlet jerkin working in a group of men uniformly clothed in brown, a small dot of scarlet moving about on long brown legs against the golden surface of the earth, and these things, intensely perceived as never before since she could remember, filled her with a piercing joy. The cold metallic gleam of halberds moving forward under a steely sky against the background of the russet woods, as a band of soldiers passed her by; the very feel and pattern of the frost upon the threshold early in the morning as the season advanced; the motion and songs of birds, until their numbers diminished; and then the iron sound of the churchbell ringing in somber majesty across the cold valleys—all these she noticed and enjoyed as never before. And even, when winter had closed around them, one night from a far-off hillside, the crying of wolves had filled her with a pleasure enhanced with dread, for the doors were safely closed and all the animals safe within walls, and a good fire roared in the great fireplace, spreading shifting constellations of gold against the black throat of the chimney, so that the dread was a luxury, and her enjoyment of the strange distant voices all the greater. And all this vividness of feeling, this new awareness of the life around her, was because of her love for this new Martin Guerre, and because of the delight and health of her life-giving body. Yet even this love was intensified, like her pleasure in the cry of the wolves, by the persistent illusion, or suspicion, that this man was not Martin.

The illusion, if such it was, did not pass away at the termination of her pregnancy, as he had prophesied it would do, but she had grown used to it. It lent a strange savor to her passion for him. Her happiness, and the happiness of her children, especially that of the newly born, the son of the new Martin, shone the more brightly, was the more greatly to be treasured because of the shadow of sin and danger which accompanied it. She wrapped the little body in swaddling bands, sheltering the little bald head from the chill spring air with her softest woolen cloth, and walked out into the fields along paths still wet from melting snow, where the earliest spring blossoms had already pricked the dead leaves. The winter wheat showed its point of new sharp green, and the air alternately misted, showered, and shone in confusing variability.

In June the wheat was harvested and the brook of the valley was turned loose by irrigating ditches upon the stubble fields, which had already begun to parch and burn in the midsummer heat. The steep fields, being so flooded, were like a series of cascades and terraces, running and shining; yet the water also sank deep into the rich earth and before long the fields were bright, some with flowers and grass, some with the new crop of buckwheat. And still the happiness of Bertrande continued, accompanied always by the shadow of her suspicion, and she could no longer say:

"It will pass when I am delivered of the child."

Through the summer, little by little the shadow increased in the mind of Bertrande. In vain did she contend with it. In a thousand small ways her suspicion was strengthened, in ways so small that she was ashamed to mention them. She thought of speaking of the matter in confession, but checked herself, saying:

"The priest will think me mad." She did not say, "Or worse, he will find a way to prove that which I only suspect."

But this was in her mind, and day after day she turned aside, she doubled her tracks, like a pursued creature, trying to avoid the realization which she knew was waiting for her. But as time went on she found herself more and more surely faced with the obligation of admitting herself to be hopelessly insane or of confessing that she was consciously accepting as her husband a man whom she believed to be an impostor. If the choice had lain within her power she would undoubtedly have chosen to be mad. For days and weeks she turned aside, as in a fever, from what she felt to be the truth, declaring to her distracted soul that she was defending the safety of her children, of her household, from Uncle Pierre down to the smallest shepherd, and then at last, one morning as she was seated alone, spinning, the truth presented itself finally, coldly, inescapably.

"I am no more mad than is this man. I am imposed upon, deceived, betrayed into adultery, but not mad."

The spindle dropped to the floor, the distaff fell across her knees, and though she sat like a woman turned into stone and felt her heart freezing slowly in her bosom, the air which entered her nostrils seemed to her more pure than any she had breathed in years, and the fever seemed to have left her body. She began then quietly to array before her in this clear passionless light the facts of her situation as she must now consider it, no longer distorted through fear or shame or through the desire of the flesh. She knew that she would never again be able to pretend that this was the man whom she had married. Although she had loved him passionately and joyously, and perhaps loved him still, and although he was the father of her son, she must rid herself of him. But could she rid herself? If she asked him to go, would he go? If she were to accuse him publicly of his crime, could she prove it? And if she could not prove it, in bringing such an accusation would she not be wronging the entire family from Sanxi and herself to the least of the cousins and cousins-in-law? And what of her youngest son, the son of the impostor? Had he no claim upon her, that she should of her own free will dishonor his birth? Terror assailed her lest she be trapped inescapably, and in her profound agitation and fear she rose and paced back and forth in the long, silent room until she was fatigued and trembling. She crossed to the window, and, leaning on the high sill, looked down into the courtyard.

Dusk was gathering, an autumn dusk. The paving stones were black with damp, but by morning they would be lacy white. While she stood there, looking down, her husband rode into the yard. A boy ran to meet him, and led his horse away after he had dismounted. The smith, whose fire glowed dimly in the cold gray light, left his work for a moment to salute his master, and returned to his work, smiling and rubbing his blackened hands together; and the old housekeeper, she who had brought the réveillon to the child bride and groom, so many years ago, appeared on the doorstep, holding a cup of warm wine. The master paused on the threshold to drink the wine and thank the old woman, and Bertrande could see quite plainly the look of adoration with which she received the empty cup.

"How firmly he is entrenched," she sighed. "How firmly."

The next day, an occasion presenting itself as Martin's younger sister was praising his conduct to his wife, Bertrande ventured:

"Yes, he is very kind, very gentle. One would almost say, is this the same man who so resembled in action and in feature your father?"

"One would almost say so," assented the sister amiably.

"But I do say so," returned Bertrande. "Often I ask myself, can this man be an impostor? And the true Martin Guerre, has he been slain in the wars?"

"Mother of Heaven," replied the sister, shocked, "how can you say such a thing, even think so? It is enough to tempt the saints to anger. Oh, Bertrande, you have not said such a thing to anyone else, have you?"

"Oh, no," she answered lightly.

"Then for the love of Our Lady, never speak of it again to me or to anyone. It is unkind. Martin could consider it an insult. He might be very angry if he heard it."

"Very well," said Bertrande. "I was jesting," and she smiled, but her heart was sick.

At confession, kneeling in the stale, cold semi-darkness, her hands muffled in her black wool capuchon, her head bowed, she said, as she had long meditated but never dared:

"Father, I have believed my husband, who is now master of my house, not to be Martin Guerre whom I married. Believing this, I have continued to live with him. I have sinned greatly."

"My child," replied the voice of the priest, without indicating the least surprise, "for what reason have you suspected this man not to be the true Martin Guerre?"

"Ah, he also has suspected him," said Bertrande to herself, and her heart gave a great leap of joy, like that of an imprisoned animal who sees the way to escape.

She replied to the priest as she had replied to her husband, giving instances of his behavior which seemed to her unnatural.

"What shall I do," she besought him finally, "what shall I do to be forgiven?"

"Softly, my child," said the calm voice of the priest. "It is then for his kindness to you that you accuse him?"

"Not for his kindness, but for the manner of his kindness."

"No matter," said the priest. "It is because of a great change in his spirit. He spoke to me of this long since, being concerned for you, and it seems to me that he has been toward you both wise and gentle. Go now in peace, my daughter. Be disturbed no more."

Bertrande continued to kneel, only drawing her cloak closer about her shoulders. The cold air seemed to draw slowly through the meshes of the wool and rise from the cold stones on which she knelt. At last she replied incredulously:

"You then believe him to be no impostor?"

"Surely not," said the easy voice of the priest, warm, definite and uncomprehending. "Surely not. Men change with the years, you must remember. Pray for understanding, my daughter, and go in peace."

Slowly she got to her feet and slowly made her way through the obscurity to the doorway, pushed aside the unwieldy leather curtain, stepped outside into the freely moving air and the more spacious dusk, and descended the familiar steps.

Familiar figures passed her, greeting her as they went on into the church. She answered them as in a dream, and as in a dream took the path to her farm. She felt like one who has been condemned to solitude, whether of exile or of prison. All the circumstances of her life, the instruction of the church, her affection for her children and her kindred rose up about her in a wall implacable as stone, invisible as air, condemning her to silence and to the perpetuation of a sin which her soul had learned to abhor. She could not by any effort of the imagination return to the happy and deluded state of mind in which she had passed the first years since the return of her husband. The realization that she was again with child added to her woe, and the weight, such as she had carried before in her body joyously, now seemed the burden of her sin made actual and dragged her down at every step.

The path, turning to follow the contours of the mountainside, brought her after a time to the crest of a slope above her farm. There it lay, house, grange and stable, set about with its own orchards, its chimney smoking gently, infinitely more familiar, more her own after all these years than the house in which she had been born; yet as she looked down toward it from the hillside she thought that it was no longer hers. An enemy had taken possession of it and had treacherously drawn to his party all those who most owed her loyalty and trust. Her eyes filled with tears, and when she drew her hands away from her face, a commotion had arisen in the courtyard below. People were running about with torches, gathering into a group from which excited cries, staccato and sonorous, rose toward the hillside, and presently three figures on horseback detached themselves from the group and rode away, the hoofs ringing on the stones. She remembered then that Martin had promised to make one of a cordon for a bear hunt from the parish of Sode, and knew that these must be his neighbors come for him.

When she reached her doorway, the housekeeper greeted her.

"The Master is gone to Sode. Ah, they are fortunate to have him! He is famous as a hunter of bear." She laughed, helping Bertrande to remove her cape; and did not see that her mistress's face had been stained with tears.

The next evening as they sat together, her husband said to Bertrande:

"Why do you look at me so strangely with your lovely two-colored eyes, your lucky eyes?"

"I was wondering when you would leave me to return again to the wars."

"I have told you never, never until you cease to love me."

"I have ceased to love you. Will you go?"

Something in the quality of her voice restrained the man from jesting.

"I do not believe you," he said, courteously.

"You must believe me," she cried with passion. "I beg of you to go. You have been here too long already," and a fire kindled in the eyes which the Gascons call lucky, the eyes of hazel and green, which made her husband lean forward and look long and searchingly into her face.

At last he said:

"You are still cherishing that madness of which you spoke, long since. Can you suppose that while you believe this thing of me, I will ever leave you? That would serve only to deepen your madness and increase your suffering. Do you not understand?"

"You are intricate," she cried. "You have the subtlety of the Evil One himself."

The man straightened, and rose from his chair. When he spoke, the quality of his voice had changed completely.

"I am sorry, Madame. There are others to be considered besides yourself. School yourself, Madame, to the inevitable."

He lifted her hand to his lips, and without another word turned and left her.

"Ah," exclaimed Bertrande bitterly, "that was the true manner of Martin Guerre. He has profited well from my complaints, this impostor."

Then began for the woman a long game of waiting and scrutinizing. Some day, she told herself, he will be off his guard, some day, if I do not warn him too often, I shall catch him in his deception, and free myself of him. "Ah, Martin, Martin," she cried in her loneliness, "where are you and why do you not return?" And as she observed the man whom she now called the impostor, considered the tranquillity of his demeanor and the ease with which he accomplished all his designs, confidently winning all people to him, the terrifying thought occurred to her that his great sense of security might lie in some certain knowledge, unshared by herself or by anyone else at Artigues. Perhaps the real Martin was indeed dead. Perhaps this man had seen his body on some distant battlefield, besmeared with blood and mutilated, the face turned downward to the bloody grass.

Perhaps, and at this last thought her soul recoiled in horror, perhaps he had himself slain Martin Guerre that he might come to Artigues in perfect safety and inherit his lands.

She watched him as he sat by the fire, fatigued from

the day's work, yet playing gently with the children, holding the youngest child upon his knee, and discoursing meanwhile to Sanxi, and he did not appear a monster. The priest came still, through the winter evenings, as before Bertrande had made her momentous confession, and, hearing the talk between the curé and the master of the house, Bertrande could not but admit that this man was wise, subtle, and, if not learnèd, infinitely skilled in argument. The priest valued him, the children loved him, and these virtues of his which entrenched him with those who should have supported her, but made her the more bitter against him. Passionate as had once been her love for this stranger, so passionate became her hatred of him, and her fear; yet in order that his power over her might not become greater, she dissembled her hatred and veiled her fear; for this reason and also because the innocent and observant eyes of Sanxi were upon her. Now all the years of loneliness before the return of Martin Guerre, or rather, before the coming of the impostor, stood her in good stead. She enclosed in her heart a single fierce determination, and outwardly her life went on as usual.

Still, she sickened. When her pallor was mentioned to her, she explained it by her physical condition. She grew more thin in cheek and shoulder as her belly grew more round. The bones of her face, the delicate arch of the nose, the high cheek bones, the wide and well-shaped skull, defined themselves under the white skin, and beneath the high arching brows her lucky eyes shone with an extraordinary luminosity.

Her husband was extremely attentive to her health, ordering all things that he could imagine to increase her comfort, excusing her from work whenever it was possible, and if there was a battle between them, apparently only Bertrande herself was aware of it. Sometimes she wondered, so unfailing were his courtesies, whether he was indeed aware of the fact that they were enemies. However, in the beginning of the spring and toward the termination of her pregnancy, an incident occurred which defined their positions beyond any doubt.

Martin's younger sister and her husband, Uncle Pierre Guerre, the curé and Martin Guerre himself, whom Bertrande called the impostor, were returning from mass at Artigues to Martin's farm. As they approached the inn, the landlord, leaning from an upper story window—for the ground floor was given over to the accommodation of the horses of his guests, according to custom—called to Martin Guerre:

"Hollah, Master Guerre, here is a friend of yours from Rochefort, an old comrade in arms who asks the way to your house."

He drew in his head, turning around to speak to a person in the room behind him, and as Martin's party came up to the door of the inn, there issued from that door a thick-set figure wearing a coat of link armor over a red woolen jerkin, who carried a cross-bow slung over one shoulder and a short sword fastened to his belt. His face was scarred from more than battle wounds, and one eye was clouded by some kind of infection that was gradually masking the lens.

"I was at Luchon," he said, coming close to them, without hesitation, "soaking my old carcass and my scabby hide in that unspeakable mud. It smells of bad eggs, pah, but it is warm, and that feels good. There I learned of your being home again, and I came to stretch my legs before your fire. Eh, Martin, we shall have much to say of Picardy, eh, and other matters less heroic." He laughed, thrusting his thumbs through his belt, but the man whom he addressed neither laughed nor smiled but regarded him with a somewhat puzzled countenance.

"Eh, Martin?" repeated the soldier, and, indicating by a nod of his head Martin's younger sister, "Is this your wife?"

"My friend of Rochefort," said Martin slowly, "I cannot for the life of me remember when or where we met. I am not so certain that we ever met at all."

The soldier cocked his head to one side, and then, with the gesture of a man who feels the leg of a spavined horse, bent quickly, and grasping Martin below the left knee, gave the leg a sharp squeeze and then a slap. Straightening himself abruptly, he announced:

"Certainly, you do not remember me! You are not even sure you know me, eh? Impostor! You are Monsieur Martin Guerre, my friend? You return from the mass, you are neat and proper, you have a great distaste for the smelly old soldier! You are nothing but a fraud. The true Martin Guerre—I knew him very well. There was a man. He could see beyond the dirt on the face of a friend. He lost a leg before St. Quentin in the year fifty-seven."

There was a dead silence, during which Martin Guerre lifted his left eyebrow the while he contracted the right, a trick, as his sister remembered, which had been characteristic of his father.

Then Uncle Pierre said:

"Brute! You have the manners of a pig. Take yourself away before you force me to roll you in the dirt."

"I do not go away so easily," said the soldier from Rochefort.

The man whom he had accused still regarded him calmly, and slowly remarked:

"Doubtless he wishes me to bribe him to leave. I have heard that there was employed under the Duke of Savoy a man who resembled me greatly in feature. Perhaps it was he who lost a leg."

"Ventre de Dieu," exclaimed the soldier with increased impatience and scorn. "I knew him well, the true Martin Guerre. He was a Gascon and he lost his left leg at the battle of St. Laurent before St. Quentin. It is all one to me if this man is a rogue. He is your relative, not mine. If he had been Martin Guerre, he would have known me."

And with many oaths he turned back to the inn, of which all the windows now stood wide open as those within tried to see and hear what went on; he was still cursing under his breath and in more languages than one as he disappeared within the shadow of the doorway, but he made no further effort to have his story believed.

"He is malicious," said Pierre Guerre with indignation, as the small party proceeded on the way to the farm.

"He was disappointed," said Martin. "He thought to find a welcome with good lodging and food for a week. I do not grudge him the food, but I cannot have him sitting about every evening telling stories of gallant adventures—which I did not commit—before my wife, who is so sick."

The curé said nothing, but Martin's sister and uncle

discussed the matter of having the soldier apprehended.

"Let it pass," said Martin. "It was a mistake; there is truly a man who resembles me. I have heard of him more than once. And the fellow was disappointed. Had he been less foul with disease I would have brought him home with us anyway, to hear the news from Spain." To the priest he added, "I could wish that this had not happened."

The priest nodded, said nothing, but the sister continued indignant and voluble, and when they reached the farm, and found Bertrande waiting for them in the kitchen, she burst at once into an account of the adventure.

"Imagine it," exclaimed Uncle Pierre as the young woman paused for breath. "Only imagine it! He leaned over, this pig of a man, and pinched Martin below the knee as if he had been a horse for sale at the market. I wonder that he did not offer to look at his teeth."

"He called Martin a rogue," repeated the sister, ever more indignant.

"Worse than that," said the brother-in-law. "He called Martin an impostor."

Bertrande, looking from one hot, excited face to another, turned at last her brilliant eyes full upon her husband's quiet countenance, in a look of triumph and scorn.

"At last," she cried suddenly in a strange hoarse voice, "at last, dear God, Thou wilt save me!"

She pressed her hands to her temples, then turned, and ran from the room.

"Go with her," said Martin, his face immediately full of concern. "Go with her quickly, my sister. Do you not see? She is ill." To the priest he said, "You understand to what a pass it has come? I would give half my farm if this soldier from Rochefort had never come to Luchon. This will unsettle her reason."

The sister, who had followed Bertrande, found her kneeling beside the bed, clutching the coverlet in agony. To all questions and reproaches she answered only:

"I am dying, I am dying. I beg of you, send for my nurse."

She was delivered that night in great suffering of a daughter who died before she had lived an hour. Bertrande herself was very ill, and in the fever which followed the birth of the child, asked only to see the soldier from Rochefort. To humor her, for he thought her hours were numbered, the curé sent for the soldier, but the man was not to be found. He had not lingered at Artigues. He had been seen at St. Gaudens some days later. After that all trace of him was lost. However, the curé caused to be written down and properly witnessed and signed the accounts of those who heard the soldier's accusation, and these papers he brought to the invalid. Immediately after she had received them, the condition of Madame Guerre began to improve, a fact which could not fail to impress not only the curé but her entire family.

"She is mad," they said to each other, "but if we humor her and are patient, God willing, she may recover."

The improvement continued. She gained strength slowly but steadily and was soon able to walk about a little in her room, but she refused steadily to leave the Chamber. She refused likewise to see her husband, to admit him to her room, or in any way to have anything to do with him. Everyone on the farm could see how heavily this weighed upon the master. He was as patient as ever with his people, and as kind, but there was little merriment.

"Madame is not herself since her illness," the housekeeper said to the priest, "and it is breaking the Master's heart."

The priest sought out Martin Guerre, and found him at work in the fields. Together they sat down in the shade of the beech trees, and the priest said:

"Who would have thought that kindness could have worked so much sorrow!"

Martin shook his head.

"There would have been no sorrow, Father, if I had not tried to run away from my father's anger. The trouble begins there. But what shall I do to help her? Once she asked me to leave her."

The priest surveyed his friend intently. If this man were not indeed his friend and the son of his friend, surely his eyes would betray him.

"And you refused to leave?" the priest said.

"At that time I refused," said the man before him, evenly, his sad eyes meeting those of the priest without hesitation. "I thought that to leave her then would but confirm her in this madness, and that I should be deserting her to years of pain—as if I were to fasten upon her the guilt of a sin—" he hesitated—"a sin of which she must not be accused."

His voice was vehement, and he stopped speaking abruptly, overcome with emotion. To the priest, who knew the voice, who knew the face, there could be no doubt whatever but that the grief, the concern and the humility were real. He passed a hand over his forehead and looked away toward the empty wheat field.

"My son," he answered at last, "I do not know what to advise you. What you have said is true. If you run away —if you disappear again—it will look like an admission of guilt. Unless, of course, you go with my consent and knowledge, leaving word of where you may be found, and denying the accusation of the fellow from Rochefort. It is conceivable that your absence might improve the condition of your wife. Your presence but adds continual fuel to the fire. The spirit is ill, and it has need of rest to heal itself, of rest as well as prayer. But you cannot leave the farm indefinitely. Your people have need of you. The parish, also—I have need of you. Is there no journey you could make about some business of the farm?"

Martin shook his head.

"The business of the farm is all in the parish of Artigues."

"You left a sum of money with your uncle when you were a boy. I think that it has never been spent. Take it, and journey to Toulouse and there purchase a gift for Our Lady. Be home again before the snow. Say farewell to your wife before you go."

"She will not speak to me," said the man with a wry smile. "But I shall say farewell to you before I go. I must help them with the wheat harvest before I leave. Meanwhile"—he hesitated—"let us say nothing of the matter until it is accomplished. There will be less talk."

The priest nodded, and blessed him. Martin Guerre returned to his work.

A few days later Bertrande herself sent for Pierre

Guerre. The honest man found her seated in the high-backed chair near the curtained bed, but as he approached her, she rose.

"I have sent for you, my uncle," she said in a low voice, "because you are still the head of our family, and I must beseech your help."

The room was cool, and to the diminished vitality of the invalid it seemed even cold. She stood wrapped in her black wool capuchon, the hood thrown back on her shoulders. Her illness had aged her, but there showed in her face such poise and clarity of spirit that the uncle was unaccountably moved.

"Sit down, my child," he said gently. "You will tire yourself."

She shook her head.

"I ask you to believe me, believe me at last, when I say to you now, 'I am not mad.' All my household believe me to be mad. I have only yourself to whom to look for help."

"I believe you, my child," he answered quietly. "Sit down. Look, I will sit down beside you on the coffer."

"I have no proof," said she, "unless the story of the soldier from Rochefort can be considered proof."

"It is a strange story," replied the uncle. "I was angered that day, but since then, the picture seems to move, like people changing places in a dance. If there is another man who resembles Martin, this must be the man. You are Martin's wife, and you would be the first to know. Moreover, he has behaved strangely of late."

"In what manner?" said Bertrande.

"He came to me demanding a sum of money which he left with me before he ran away. I replied that the money had made part of the sum for the purchase of the lower fields. It was a matter of which his father had approved. The purchase was made after his father's death, according to his father's plan."

"I remember," said Bertrande. "What then?"

"He was angered," said Pierre shortly.

"I understand," said Bertrande slowly. "He wishes money in hand in order to leave us. Now that he fears detection, now that he has pillaged us, now that he has almost killed me, he will go away." She began to weep and hid her face in her hands.

A deliberate, abiding wrath grew in the old uncle as he watched her bent head and listened to her sobs. "Madame," he said, striking with his clenched hand upon his knee, "give me your permission to accuse this man of his crime. He shall not leave us unpunished."

Bertrande could hardly speak for her tears. But:

"Accuse him, punish him, do as you like with him, only rid me of his presence," she implored.

Less than a week later armed men from Rieux arrived at the farm and arrested the master of the house. They brought him in irons from the field to the kitchen for a final identification by Bertrande. His own men followed after, angry and sullen. Standing beside the master's chair, before the hearth, Bertrande identified him as the man who had claimed, but falsely, to be her husband.

"I accuse him," she said clearly, "of being an impostor and not the true Martin Guerre."

It was the first time since the birth of the child that she had left her room. Uncle Pierre stood beside her. It was evident that the men from Rieux had been expected.

Sanxi, seeing his father in chains, burst into a passion of weeping, flung himself, first upon his father, and then, kicking and scratching, upon the two guardsmen.

"Madame," said his father quietly, above the turmoil thus raised, "is it indeed you who do this to me?"

Bertrande bowed her head, and turned her back upon him.

The man sighed, and nodded, as if to himself. Then, turning to the housekeeper, he asked that the youngest child be brought. The old woman, all in tears, held up the little one to his father to be kissed. The people of the farm crowded about, and the priest, entering in haste, cried to the men-at-arms:

"This is folly—you do not know what you are doing!" He stretched out his hands and would have prevented their departure.

"Let be," said the prisoner, still quietly. "It is not the fault of the men. They must do as they have been commanded." And then, addressing his people, he said: "Good-by, my children. God willing, I shall return to you safely."

"It is a mistake," said the priest again to the guardsmen. "You do not understand that the woman is mad."

But the guard moved forward, with the prisoner between them, through the wide doorway into the courtyard of the farm. The housekeeper, Sanxi and the other servants followed closely behind them. There was some delay in the courtyard as a horse was brought for the prisoner. Bertrande, who had continued to stand with her back to the room, her eyes upon the hearth, turned now and looked about her. She was entirely alone. In the courtyard the servants shouted their last farewells. She heard Sanxi's voice.

"Good-by, my father, my dear father!"

II. RIEUX

The accusation had been made at Rieux, since Artigues was too small a place to boast a court, and thither Bertrande went with her uncle, Pierre, and the servants who were to be called as witnesses. She stayed in the house of her mother's sister, occupying the same room which she had been given on her earlier visit, and in which the sun had always seemed to shine through western windows in the morning. But this time the sun shone from the east, as it should do, and Bertrande marveled that she had ever felt confused about the direction. In the same fashion she marveled that she should have permitted herself to be deceived concerning the identity of the man who had called himself her husband. Her present belief was inescapable and plain, and yet she found herself alone in it, alone, that is, save for the support of honest Pierre. She left in Artigues a house in which the very servants looked at her askance. Of Martin's four sisters, two had not hesitated to declare that they thought her malicious. They said openly, so that the report returned to her:

"For years during Martin's absence she was sole mistress of the farm. Now she cannot bear to be put back into her proper place. She has a greed of authority, and of money. She was severe to us before we married, severe and miserly. This is all a plan to destroy Martin and possess the farm."

The other sisters, particularly the youngest, defended her. She had done no more in the management of the estate and of the family than their mother would have required her to do, and her strange fancy that Martin was not her husband had arisen from the grief of the long separation. They were sure that she was insane. The charity and the coldness were alike difficult for Bertrande; and at Rieux, even her aunt supported the claim of the impostor.

"My poor child," she said to Bertrande, "your years of suffering have told on your brain in a strange way. Why, I have known the boy all his life! Of course I shall testify in his favor, if I am asked, and when the courts have decided that he is really your husband, perhaps you will have some peace, although it's all a great pother to go through with in order to convince a wife of what she ought to know without help."

At the first session of the court the crime was formally charged to the prisoner of misrepresentation and theft. Bertrande then demanded through Pierre Guerre, and in fact only because of the uncle's insistence, that the prisoner be made to do penance publicly, that he pay a fine to the king, and that he pay to herself the sum of ten thousand livres. She was then asked to state her reasons for the accusation.

"My lords," she began, "there is the testimony of the soldier from Rochefort."

She was interrupted.

"We ask you for your testimony only," they reminded her.

She bent her head, and after a moment, told them just what she had told the priest. Upon being questioned further, she added:

"I also found it curious, upon remarking the prisoner at sword practice with my son, that Martin Guerre should fence so awkwardly; he was known to be distinguished in the art."

The prisoner smiled, and shrugged his shoulder slightly. A brief smile also flitted across the face of one of the judges, and Bertrande, seeing it, exclaimed:

"You may smile, my lord, and my testimony may seem innocent to you and of small importance, but I swear by God and all His holy angels that this man is not my husband. Of that I am certain, though I should die for it."

"Well, we shall inquire, Madame, we shall inquire," said the justice, and called for the accused to be examined.

The prisoner stepped forward with an easy manner, as if he stood before his own hearth. He explained that during his absence he had served the King of Spain, that he had traveled extensively both through Spain and France, and that he had not known until he came to Rieux, some three years earlier, that his parents were dead; that upon learning that he was head of the house, he had made all haste to return to his wife and child, and had endeavored in every way to make up for his past neglect. He furnished the names and addresses of people who could verify the story of his wanderings. He told of his return to Artigues, of how Pierre Guerre, his uncle, had been the first person in the village to recognize and welcome him, and averred that Pierre had been to him in all things friendly until he, Martin, had found reason to question Pierre about the disposition of a certain sum of money which he had left in the care of his uncle. Since that time, he said, his uncle had sought to destroy him. He even hinted in conclusion that an attempt had been made upon his life.

The judges then asked him a great number of questions regarding the history of his family, the date of his own wedding, the date of birth of Sanxi, to all of which he answered without hesitation.

"Madame," said the judges to Bertrande, "you have heard these answers. Are they correct?"

"They are all correct, my lords," said Bertrande, "but still the man is not my husband."

The judges conferred together and presently announced that the case would be dismissed for a short time while an examination should be made into the characters of the accusers. Bertrande, her face burning with shame at this implication, turned to Martin's uncle.

"This is because we have asked for money," she said bitterly. "All that I ask, all that I hope is to be rid of his presence."

Uncle Pierre shrugged his shoulders.

"You must not be unreasonable," he told her. "After all, there will be the expense of the trial."

However, the investigation determined that the characters of Bertrande and Pierre were above reproach, and the case was ordered to proceed. In the interval, word of the dispute had gone round the countryside, and a great number of persons had either presented themselves voluntarily or had been called by the court as witnesses. On the morning when the case reopened, the chambers of the judges were crowded with interested persons, of whom no fewer than one hundred and fifty were present in the quality of witnesses.

The examination of relatives began, followed by that of the farm servants, then of neighbors from Artigues. Without a dissenting voice they all declared that the man in fetters was no other than Martin Guerre himself. The priest, being called, declared that the man was Martin and gave an eloquent account of Bertrande's illness and her madness, as he had discussed it with her husband and herself.

The day was wearing to a close, and Bertrande, sadly, said to Pierre Guerre:

"Do not all these people begin to convince you that you may be mistaken?"

"I am not one to change my mind every five minutes," said honest Pierre. "I have thought him a rogue, and a rogue he remains."

The priest departed and a new witness was called.

"Your name?" said the judge.

"Jean Espagnol."

"And whence do you come?"

"From Tonges, my lord."

"Your occupation?"

"Soldier of fortune."

"Do you know the prisoner?"

"That I do, my lord."

"And by what name do you know him?"

"Arnaud du Tilh, my lord. Sometimes we call him Pansette."

A murmur ran over the room. People stretched themselves, and Bertrande shot a glance at the accused man, whose face, however, showed no guilt, no surprise and only a very natural interest in the proceeding.

"And how long have you known the prisoner?"

"Oh, from the cradle, my lord."

"Have you had any conversation with him of late?"

"My lord, he told me less than half a year ago that he was playing the part of one Martin Guerre, that he had met this said Guerre in the wars, and that this Guerre made over to him, for certain considerations, the whole of his estate and the permission to impersonate himself."

"Ah, it is a lie," cried the voice of Bertrande, passionately.

"Well said, Madame," added the prisoner.

"Silence," demanded the judge.

The witness spread his hands palm outwards with the expression of a man who has done his best for the cause of truth and justice, and, being dismissed, took his place again in the crowd.

From then on the case began to appear most dubious for the prisoner, for although it was rather a tall story that Martin Guerre would have made over all his possessions to a wandering rogue for whatever considerations, there were many witnesses examined who declared that the prisoner was in fact a Gascon by the name of Arnaud du Tilh. There were also among the witnesses called, some who were acquainted with both Martin Guerre and the rogue du Tilh. Of these, some said that the prisoner was Martin, some that he was Arnaud, and some declared themselves unable to decide between the two. The examination of witnesses ran on at such length that it was necessary to reconvene the court on the following day. Finally, when the last witness had given his testimony, the judges sent for Sanxi, and tried to find in his face some resemblance to the man who claimed to be his father. But since the boy so obviously resembled his father's sisters, who were said to resemble their mother, rather than their father, the countenance of Sanxi was of little aid to the judges.

The judges withdrew and debated the case at length. Bertrande, sitting clasping and unclasping her hands, overheard two of the spectators who were commenting freely on the case. Said one:

"They have proved nothing against the man, and the woman demands a great sum of money."

"If she denies him to be her husband," said the other, "why did she not deny it immediately? She lived with him for three years without complaining. Why does she quarrel with him now?"

"She has lost her pains, without a doubt," said the first.

"My God, my God," said Bertrande, bowing her head and clasping and unclasping her long hands in a passion of despair, "deliver me from sin."

The judges returned and prepared to speak:

"Whereas, out of one hundred and fifty witnesses called by this court of Rieux, forty have testified that the prisoner is Martin Guerre, sixty have refused to testify to his identity, and fifty have testified that he is none other than Arnaud du Tilh, and whereas the wife of Martin Guerre, whose opinion should bear more weight with us than that of any other living person, has testified that the prisoner is not her husband, we do affirm that the prisoner is in fact Arnaud du Tilh, commonly known as Pansette. And we do condemn the said Arnaud du Tilh to do public penance before the church of Artigues, and before the house of Martin Guerre, and to suffer death by decapitation before the house of Martin Guerre."

A gasp as of astonishment and pity swept the room, and Bertrande de Rols, rising from her seat, cried out in a clear, terrified voice:

"Not death! Not death! No, no, I have not demanded his death!"

She stood, grown very pale, confronting the judges with surprise and horror in her features; and then, putting out her hand gropingly, she half-turned toward Pierre Guerre, and fell unconscious into his arms.

The prisoner had started also at Bertrande's cry. In spite of the sentence just passed upon him, his eyes were clear, and his face bright, one would have said, with joy.

III. TOULOUSE

It is difficult to relate all that Bertrande de Rols suffered in the days which followed directly upon this decision. She returned to Artigues, to a house in which all peace and contentment had been destroyed. Nor was there anyone in Artigues, except Martin's uncle, who did not by word or gesture blame her for this destruction. Sanxi regarded her with frightened, incredulous eyes, or slipped from a room as she entered, like a small animal who has been beaten continuously and without having offended. Nor was the matter ended. If the sentence had been carried through without delay, Bertrande felt, she might have borne the horror with some courage and reached, afterwards, a certain peace of finality, and time might have justified her action; but the case had been appealed at once by Martin's sisters to the parliament of Toulouse, and the summer dragged forward through a long, heartbreaking uncertainty.

The wheat was harvested, but without exultation, and threshed, but without merriment. As in other years the water of the mountain stream was turned upon the stubble fields and ran in shining cascades across the parched and broken earth, but Bertrande de Rols did not walk out to see it, nor did it matter to her that the flowers sprang up after the passage of the water as if a carpet had suddenly been spread, a carpet of a thousand flowers and a thousand pleasant odors. During the last days of August word was brought to Artigues that the parliament of Toulouse had found the evidence inconclusive and had called the witnesses for a second trial.

The curé visited Bertrande.

"My daughter," he said, as persuasive and kindly as if she had not now for almost a year steadily refused his advice, "it is no more than my duty to entreat you to consider once more that which you have undertaken."

"Reverend Father," said Bertrande abruptly, "have you never once thought but that I might be right? Consider the soldier from Rochefort. Is it not possible that this man may indeed be Arnaud du Tilh? Is it not more than likely?"

"All things are possible with God," said the priest, "but I cannot think it likely that the man of whom we speak should be one and the same with a most notorious rogue." His voice softened and his eyes became very sad. "The man of whom we speak was one whom I had grown to value greatly. His ways, his thoughts, were kindly. There was no soul in my parish of Artigues who did not benefit in some way from his presence here."

"You valued him," said Bertrande quietly, "more than you valued Martin Guerre who ran away?"

"Indeed, more," said the priest. "What was that boy? A raw, impatient youth, a thoughtless boy, selfish in the extreme. He had in him, it is true, the qualities of a great man. I like to think that he has grown into that man. His selfishness has become generosity, his impatience has become energy well-directed. It did not happen suddenly. He was eight years in a hard school." He paused, and in a curious voice asked her, "It does not pain you to hear me praise him?"

"No," she answered slowly, as if she questioned herself. "It is no more than just to remember that he has been kind to us—kind to all, save me, and kind even to me after a strange fashion."

"Then if it does not pain you to hear him praised," said the priest, pursuing his slight advantage, "if it pleases you a little to hear good of him, then you cannot have ceased entirely to love him, and does not this love convince you that he is truly Martin Guerre?"

"No," said Bertrande fiercely and quickly. "No, Father. Can you not see, it is in this love that he has wronged me most, that he has damned my soul? I have sinned, through him, and you will not understand it even long enough to give me absolution! No, Father, I cannot believe him to be other than the rogue, Arnaud du Tilh."

Her cheeks had flushed, as if with a fever, and to the priest her eyes held a strange luminosity. He lifted his hand and then, helplessly, dropped it upon his knee. He said:

"There is a doubt, nevertheless. While there remains a doubt you run the risk of unwillingly, unwittingly, assisting at the destruction of your own husband. I counsel you to withdraw the charges before it is too late. Those who love you, and him, have given you an opportunity of retreating from this whole affair.

"Is it for you to assume vengeance? You believe that you have sinned. You are in danger of sinning far more greatly. If there is evil in the matter, God will unravel it in His own good time. No, do not answer now. I advise you to withdraw the accusation. If you cannot do this, if your heart will not permit you to do this, then I shall pray for you that you may be prevented against your will from so harming, not only yourself, but all who love you."

He left her sorely shaken, as he had meant to do, not in her opinion of the man's guilt, but in her belief in the wisdom of her action. The event had gone beyond her plan. "I did not demand his death," she reminded herself; "but now I must demand it."

After the priest came Martin's youngest sister. She knelt in front of Bertrande and, covering Bertrande's two hands with her own, looked up into the face of her sister-in-law, and said most pleadingly:

"Bertrande, my dearest sister, we were always good friends. Do not be angry with me now. When you come before the judges of Toulouse, say to them, 'I withdraw the charges made against my husband. I do not know how it happened—I think that I was mad.' Our uncle will not press the charges, if you do not. Martin will forgive you. We shall all be happy again. Dear God," and she suddenly began to weep, "we cannot have him killed before his own house."

She bowed her head on her hands, and Bertrande felt upon her own cold fingers the warm tears.

"Little sister," she answered in despair, "how can I deny the truth?"

"It is only the truth for you, not for us," returned the weeping girl. "For the truth, that none of us believe, you would destroy us all. We shall never be happy again. The farm will never prosper again."

"Your uncle believes as I do," said Bertrande.

"Ah, but he is old. He wants nothing to be changed that was not just as it was when our father died. He would not change a cobble stone. And Martin changes everything, and is changed himself, so that we all love him more."

"Well, then," said Bertrande, "if the man be Martin, as you would have me say, why does not Arnaud du Tilh come forward and declare himself? Why should he let an innocent man suffer in his name?"

"He has enough to answer for with the law," replied the girl with some impatience. "It is to his advantage to be considered dead. The law will cease to seek for him. And why should a rogue put his neck into a halter for the sake of another?"

Bertrande sighed and laid her hand gently on the girl's shoulder.

"I am so sorry," she said, "so sorry." But she promised nothing.

September came, reddening the vines, making the mornings and evenings cool. Bertrande, returning from church the evening before her departure, whither she had gone in preparation for the journey to Toulouse, crossed the courtyard toward her house, wearily. She saw the housekeeper sitting near the doorway killing doves, and sat down beside the old woman.

"You have made your prayers, Madame," said the old woman.

"Yes."

"I wish that you had made them for a better cause."

"How can you know what prayers I made?"

"I cannot know, Madame. I only know that since you have had this strange idea of yours, nothing goes well for us. And all was well before. So well."

She sighed, leaning forward, holding the dove head down between her hands, the smooth wings folded close to the smooth soft body, while the dark blood dripped slowly from a cut in the throat into an earthen dish. The dish, already filled with blood, darker than that which was falling into it, spilled over slightly, and a barred gray cat, creeping cautiously near, elongated, its belly close to the ground, put out a rasping pale tongue and licked the blood. The housekeeper, after a little, pushed it away with the side of her foot. A pile of soft gray-feathered bodies already lay beside her on the bench. The living dove turned its head this way and that, struggled a little, clasping a pale cold claw over the hand that held it, and relaxed, although still turning its head. The blood seemed to be clotting too soon, the wound was shrunken, and the old woman enlarged it with the point of the knife which she had in her lap. The dove made no cry. Bertrande watched with pity and comprehension the dying bird, feeling the blood drop by drop leave the weakening body, feeling her own strength drop slowly away like the blood of the dove.

"What would you have me do?" she asked at length. "The truth is only the truth. I cannot change it, if I would."

The old woman turned her head without lifting her shoulders, still leaning forward heavily above her square, heavy lap. Her face was much more lined than in the days when Bertrande had first known her. There were creases above and below her lips, parallel with the line of the lips, as well as creases at the corners of the mouth. Her forehead was scored with lines that arched one above the other regularly, following the arches of the eyebrows. There were fine radiating lines about her eyes. The skin was brown and healthy, with ruddy patches on the cheek bones, but nevertheless the face was worn.

"I, Madame?" she said.

Bertrande looked into the tired affectionate brown eyes and nodded.

"Ah," said the housekeeper, turning once more to the dove which now lay still in her hands, "Madame, I would have you still be deceived. We were all happy then." She laid the dead dove with the others, and stooped to pick up the dish of blood.

All the way to Toulouse the echoes of these three conversations rang through the mind of Bertrande de Rols, making a slow, confused accompaniment to the clop-clop of the horses' hooves. The housekeeper rode behind her, Uncle Pierre before. They descended the valley of the Neste, the road running close to the stream, until the valley closed about them narrowly, leaving barely room for the passage of the torrent and the path above it. The woods were yellowing, but were still rich in leafy shadow. They came from the deep gorge to the wider valley of the Garonne, the stream coming in swiftly from the right, from the valley of Aran, saw St. Bertrand de Comminges with its narrow buttresses rising from its stony pedestal far below them in the green cup of the hills, crossed the Garonne and came into the more spacious country where the heavy-laden vines were trained from maple tree to maple tree in natural festoons. They passed St. Gaudens and St. Martory; they approached Muret. It was the journey which Bertrande had taken in imagination with Martin that autumn when he had first left her, and it was all rich and lovely, the wild mountain scenery giving way gradually to more thickly clustered farms, thorn hedges around the autumn gardens, and fruit trees set about the houses, medlars, plums and cherries, and always the fresh running of the water beyond the road; but now she traveled in great bitterness of heart, hearing through the noise of the hooves and the splashing of the Garonne, only the reproaches and prayers of those dependent upon her.

It had come to be a fixed idea with her that Martin was dead. It was incredible to her that any man could stand so calmly to face the extravagant charges brought against him as Arnaud du Tilh had done, if he had not certain knowledge that the man was dead whose place he usurped. Justly or unjustly she believed also that du Tilh had had something to do with Martin's death. Being so bereaved, and so unjustly blamed, herself, she would have welcomed almost any plan that would have given her back the sympathy and understanding of those she loved. And they had entreated her to withdraw the charges against du Tilh. Well, and if she did? Was it too late? Might she not restore to them the happier days?

"I, Madame? I could wish you still to be deceived."

The words recurred to her again and again. Might she not purchase for her people with this one secret weight of shame against her soul the peace and happiness which she desired for them and for herself their forgiveness and gratitude?

Again, if the court of Toulouse should reverse the decision of the court of Rieux, what then? Might she not feel released from this necessity of pursuit and revenge? The judges of Toulouse were very learnèd men and very near to the king in authority. The king, in turn, was appointed of God. Might she not consider it in some sense an indication from heaven, if the court should command her to receive this man as her husband, and might she not thereby find peace?

She had not seen the man whom she accused since the day in court when she had cried out against the sentence of death. His face had grown a little shadowy, the whole quality of his person a little unreal. Riding in the late afternoon under the shadow of trees, and out from that shadow into the light of a meadow, then again into the shadow of other, farther trees, she let herself slip for a time into a dream of surrender, and drooping over the saddle-bow, giving herself easily to the slow motion of the horse, she thought only of the restored tranquillity in the big kitchen, the contented faces bent above the evening meal—little of the man seated in the chair by the hearth, and, for the time being, nothing of herself in that new and impossible relationship. Meanwhile Pierre Guerre rode before her, and when she lifted her eyes from the roadway, or from the contemplation of the roadside grass, she saw his broad and honest back going steadily on.

She remembered then that he was not only her one supporter in the task which she had undertaken, but that he was also the one remaining defender of the old authority of her husband's house. He was that authority, simple and direct, without need of subterfuge or of superfluous charm, which before the coming of the stranger had kept them all in a secure and wholesome peace. He was for her that day a tradition more potent than the church. In her country the church had sometimes been denied, but even the Albigenses, hunted from town to town, from town to mountain cavern, and mercilessly destroyed for that denial, had never denied the tradition of which Pierre Guerre was the symbol. When she lay down that night in a strange bed in a strange valley, it was with a fatigue which overwhelmed body and soul, so that she felt she would have been fortunate never to waken.

On the third day of their journey they had come to the lowlands, and the September heat was excessive. There were no more cool ravines with belated shadows, where the water dripped from rocks, and where ferns grew. Now the fields lay parched and dusty. A white dust rose constantly from the road under the horses' hooves, and the leaves of the plane trees were dulled by dust. Earlier in the day they traversed the waste lands, filled with rocks and patches of wild lavender. At noon the heat was so great that they stopped to rest for nearly three hours under a grove of plane trees. Here there was shade for them and for their beasts, but the cicadas, boring into the bark of the trees for cooling drinks in the hot weather, beat their cymbals so loud in their great content, at the heat, at the sweet liquid which they sucked all day, that the whole grove rang, harshly reverberant. The air seemed to tremble to the sound, and for Bertrande they were a torment made audible. She was glad to resume the way, although the noise of the cicadas accompanied them still, now near, now far, as they passed other groves.

The Garonne ran, broader now, no longer splashing and sparkling, but sullenly, a yellow flood weighted with earth from the mountain-sides where the goats browsed. They crossed it toward evening over a wooden bridge into the city of Toulouse. Farther downstream, the first four arches of the Pont Neuf, the new stone bridge which was to be so well and so cleverly constructed that it would withstand even the most violent of the spring floods, projected its incompleted ramp less than half way across the yellow tide. Before them on the quay, the western sunlight shone full upon the whitened brick façade of Notre Dame de la Dalbade, and behind them the Pyrenees, of which a long spur had accompanied them almost to the city, retreated range upon snowy range, now turning slowly rose-color, far away, even into Spain. Behind La Dalbade lay Toulouse, a huddle of buildings of a dusty, rose-colored brick, intricate, noisy and odorous. The mountain peasants crossed the quay, passed the white façade of the church, and plunged into the network of echoing streets.

They found an inn and ordered supper, after engaging lodging for the night. The ordinary was full of guests, mostly merchants from the neighboring small towns, with a sprinkling of city men. Bertrande found a place in a corner, and, leaning back against the stained plastered wall, took refuge from herself and her companions in the public confusion of the room. Gradually, through the fog of personal misery which enveloped her, she observed that the talk was not general and easy, as one might have expected it to be, but that a group of men was giving great attention to a small number of travelers, and that there was a great deal of head-shaking, and of sober looks. When the hostess brought her supper, she detained her long enough to ask of what the men were talking.

"Of Amboise Madame. You have heard nothing of Amboise?"

Bertrande shook her head.

"You are Catholic, Madame?"

Bertrande nodded.

"And so am I, Madame, but Amboise was the work of

the Guises. God be praised, we have no such Catholics in Toulouse. It seems there was a conspiracy of a sort, not greatly proved—there was more talk than evidence. And for that—every kind of death: hangings, decapitations, drownings, without number every day, and so for a whole month. I am Catholic like yourself, Madame, but in Toulouse for every Catholic there is at least one Protestant. And they are good people, Madame. I promise you, I would as soon cut off my own head as that of my neighbor, and that for his being merely a Protestant!"

"But judging from those faces," said Pierre Guerre, indicating the talkers on the other side of the room, "one would think it a rebellion sooner than a conversation."

"A rebellion, yes," said the hostess. "I would not think it impossible. Toulouse has not always been bound to the French crown."

She went off, and the somber discussion continued, never more animated, never less intense, like a storm cloud that hangs patiently at the edge of an horizon, waiting for a wind to blow it into action.

"I do not know what is the matter with the world," said Pierre Guerre. "It seems to be breaking up in little pieces. In the days of Francis we were strongly French."

The room in which they slept, the entire party of mountaineers, for the inn was crowded, was hot and close. In the morning the streets were still warm and in the unmoving air the odors and stenches of the previous days remained, like a kind of disembodied refuse. There was none of the early morning crispness of the mouutains, nor the amplitude of the purified air in which odors of the farm, of the beasts and of cooking, stood like symbols of the force and vigor, the healthiness of life. Bertrande awoke unrefreshed and felt in the air, as in her mind, the sultriness which paralleled the sullen temper of the men in the eating-room the evening before.

After the cup of wine, which seemed sour, and a piece of bread, which seemed bitter, she followed Pierre Guerre bare-headed through the streets to the council chambers of the Parliament in the Château Narbonnais.

The streets were crowded. People were speaking, not the mountain patois, but Languedocien, and with a curiously clanging, hard resonance, which made, in the narrower passages, everything seem to be spoken twice, re-echoed in metallic vigor from the dusty walls. And all the way Bertrande asked of herself, What am I doing here, in this unhappy town, in this prolonged stench, this heat, this desolating strangeness? I am pursuing a man to his death, a man who has been many times kind to me, who is the father of my smallest child. I am destroying the happiness of my family. And why? For the sake of a truth, to free myself from a deceit which was consuming me and killing me. She remembered herself speaking to Martin's sister.

"What would you have, my sister? The truth is only the truth. I cannot change it."

The sister had replied:

"It is true only for you."

"And might I be wrong?" she asked herself again as she mounted the stone steps and stood waiting before the great, closed door. She felt, in approaching this tribunal of Toulouse, a finality she had not felt at Rieux. It would not be possible for her to appeal this decision. It waited for her, behind those doors, in the quality of a doom. Suddenly her confidence deserted her, and terror engulfed her. She saw herself as borne forward helplessly on a great tide of misunderstanding and mischance to commit even a greater sin than that of which she had been afraid. The words of the priest returned to her. It had been holy counsel; she had refused it. She broke into a heavy sweat which turned cold on her skin and made her shudder even in the meridional heat. She was dizzied. The door before her grew insubstantial, invisible, as if she had walked into an icy cloud on the summit of La Bancanère. Blindly, she reached out her hand for Uncle Pierre, and, the doors being opened, she entered the courtroom leaning on his arm.

The judges of Toulouse wished to confront the two accusers with the accused, but singly, feeling that much might be revealed to the acute observer in the countenances of the accusers which had not been recorded in the account of the case forwarded to them by the judges of Rieux. Accordingly, once inside the courtroom, Bertrande was constrained to leave the support of Uncle Pierre, and, attended by a guard, advanced before the very seat of the judges. A hum of voices which had filled the room ceased suddenly as she appeared. In the abrupt silence she heard the admonition and then the question of the judge and, lifting her eyes, saw before her at the distance of only a few feet, the man for whom she had felt for one extraordinary year a great and joyous passion. He was regarding her with a look at once patient, tender and ironic. In her distress she saw no other face, and could not bear the contemplation of that tender gaze. She looked down, dropping her head forward, while the blood beat upward into her face and then receded. Who was this Arnaud du Tilh? What manner of man was he that he did not return her hatred with hatred, and why had he not made good his escape from this most dangerous justice on the day when she had first suspected him? Her face turned very white, while a return of the giddiness which had seized her just before she entered the court made it almost impossible for her to continue standing. She replied to the questions of the judges in a half-audible voice, and was then escorted to a small doorway through which she gained the courtyard, the sunlight, and a degree of solitude. She was instructed to return to the inn and to remain there until sent for. She went to her room and lay down.

Inside of an hour Pierre Guerre, who had been similarly instructed, joined her there. He was morose, annoyed at being detained at the inn, feeling himself a prisoner and having no occupation, large or small, with which to while away the time. He felt that he had behaved badly at the trial, and it was true that, although his conviction was as sound as ever, his manner had been hesitating, and embarrassed. He had felt himself stared at and smiled at as a peasant, a mountaineer. He had overheard, as the guard led him through the crowded room, an amused comment on his dress, the wit of which he had not understood, but the intent of which he had understood only too well. Annoyed at the crowd, humble before the judges, suddenly for the first time in his life acutely self-conscious, he had lost, for the space of five minutes, the simple dignity which had lent, at Rieux, such great weight to his testimony. Added to this discomfort was the spectacle of the impostor who had lost during his period of imprisonment some of his healthy brown color but none of his air of being arrogantly in the right.

"We are lost," said old Pierre to himself as he returned to the inn. "If it depended on me, we are lost indeed."

He dared not mention his discomfort to his niece, but it was the principal reason for the morose silence with which he rejoined her and set himself to wait out the day.

Bertrande lay upon the bed and regarded the stained canopy. Or she turned her head idly and surveyed the wall, or the figure of old Pierre seated on a straight bench under the window. She felt a great illness. A weight seemed to lie upon her breast which made breathing difficult, and the air which entered her lungs, after she had made so great an effort to expand them, contained no freshness, no reviving quality. Her mind had gone numb through prolonged self-examination. Exhausted and trapped by all these walls, by all these circumstances, she lay still and remembered that the one thing she desired was to be free of Arnaud du Tilh.

Meanwhile the court was proceeding with the examination of witnesses. One hundred and fifty witnesses had been called from the hearing at Rieux, and thirty new ones. Jean Espagnol testified as he had done at the former trial, and introduced a friend, Pelegrin de Liberos by name.

Pelegrin de Liberos, being sworn, testified that he was an old friend of Arnaud du Tilh, and that Arnaud had recently not only admitted his identity to him, but had given him a handkerchief to be delivered to Arnaud's brother, Jean du Tilh.

Gradually a body of information was built up, minute

details contributed now by one witness, now by another. The shoemaker of Artigues testified that the foot of Martin Guerre exceeded slightly that of the accused. Certain witnesses to the number of five who had formerly testified with assurance that the accused was indeed Martin Guerre, now declared that they could not be sure whether he was or whether he was not. Of the thirty new witnesses, twelve declared themselves unable to make any decision regarding the identity of the accused. He might be either Martin Guerre or Arnaud du Tilh, for all they could observe. On the other hand, seven of the new witnesses were quite sure that he was du Tilh, and ten were equally convinced that he was Martin Guerre. It was established that Martin Guerre had appeared to be taller and more slender than Arnaud du Tilh, and that he had been somewhat round-shouldered. However there was also the argument that since the accused was eleven years older than was Martin Guerre when last seen, the natural increase in weight and age might make him seem shorter than had appeared Martin Guerre, the boy of twenty.

Still, as the day went on, it was decided beyond a doubt that Martin Guerre had two teeth broken in the lower left jaw, as had also the accused; that Martin Guerre had a scar on the right eyebrow and the trace of an ulcer on one cheek, as had also the accused; that Martin Guerre had a drop of extravasated blood in the left eye, as had also the prisoner; that Martin Guerre had the nail of the left forefinger missing, and three warts on the left hand, two of which were on the little finger, as had also the man in fetters. So that the evidence tended well toward the defense, when there appeared before the judges an old man in the clothes of a mountaineer but with a somewhat more distinguished bearing than the costume might have seemed to warrant. He was sworn and his name was asked.

"I am called Carbon Bareau."

"And do you recognize the prisoner?"

"Gentlemen, this man in irons is the child of my own sister."

The old man then began to weep, and it was some time before he had recovered composure sufficient to continue.

"I have loved this boy," he said at last, "for he has a way with him, a way of stealing the heart, but I have feared for him ever since he grew old enough to talk. He has had no respect for the laws, gentlemen. It breaks my heart to say that he has even declared there is no God. He has revered his parents not at all. With no faith, no respect for family, nor for the law of the kingdom, what could one hope for, gentlemen? He has a good heart, that is all. But what is a good heart when he can so disgrace an honorable family?"

The two brothers of Arnaud du Tilh were then called and testified that the prisoner "resembled" their brother. Further than that they would not commit themselves.

After this came a long succession of witnesses for the defense, forty-five people all of blameless reputation and well-qualified to know what they were talking about. Martin's four sisters testified that the accused was their brother, as did also two brothers-in-law. Many people who had been guests at the wedding of Bertrande and Martin testified that the accused was certainly Martin Guerre. The curé of Artigues testified in favor of his friend.

Last witness of all came the old housekeeper who had

brought to the bridal couple the little midnight repast, or réveillon. She had a story to tell after she had identified the prisoner as her young master. She stood before the judges with her hands clasped firmly at her belt, her brown eyes, good, honest, kind, fixed steadily upon the revered faces, and cleared her throat. Shortly after the return of Monsieur, she testified, she had heard Madame remark to Monsieur that she had kept certain chests unopened since his departure, so long ago. Upon hearing this, Monsieur had described certain white culottes wrapped in a piece of taffeta and requested that they be fetched him. Whereupon Madame had given to the housekeeper the key to the chest and requested her to fetch the *pantalons,* and the housekeeper had done so, finding them wrapped exactly as Monsieur had described. She made her recital bravely, greatly impressed herself at the gravity with which the judges heard it, and then, trembling with triumph and embarrassment, crept back to her place.

It was now late in the afternoon. The day's heat seemed to have accumulated in the crowded room along with the testimony of the witnesses, and the place was stifling. The light which entered through the high windows struck almost levelly upon the wall opposite, above the heads of the judges. The scribe laid down his pen, and the judges leaned forward to confer with each other. The examination was over, and it remained only to interpret the information. Those who had most to lose or gain by the decision had been dismissed to an inner room, but the courtroom was still packed.

It was neither reasonable nor just, the court argued first of all, to permit the bad reputation of the rogue

Arnaud du Tilh to affect the fate of the prisoner if he was indeed Martin Guerre. Secondly, the judges argued, if it were so easy for the wife of Martin Guerre to mistake Arnaud for her husband, even if only for a short time, it would have been just as easy for the soldier from Rochefort to mistake Arnaud for Martin; there was no way of proving that the man who lost a leg at the battle of St. Laurent before St. Quentin was Martin Guerre rather than Arnaud du Tilh. Thirdly, they argued, it was beyond human ingenuity for any man to impersonate so well, to know so many intimate details of the life of another man, and to exhibit so close a physical resemblance to another man as the accused. Last of all, the court considered that the confusion of Bertrande at the sight of the accused, together with the report of her outcry in the court of Rieux when the sentence of death had been pronounced against the prisoner, testified badly for her case. Therefore the judges decided, and doubtless to their own relief, for they had been sadly puzzled, that the prisoner must be in truth none other than Martin Guerre, as he himself affirmed. The populace seemed pleased with the decision, and the clerk of the court prepared to put the verdict down in writing.

As this individual drew up his inkpot and sharpened his pen, and as the judges of Toulouse relaxed in their chairs and mopped their foreheads, conversing among themselves, and not, shrewdly, overlooking the smiles which overspread the courtroom, a commotion was heard at the outer door in which could be distinguished a great deal of stamping and of beating on the stone floor with the butt of a halberd, and a vigorous exposition of an undeterminable nature in an unmistakably Gascon voice. The court sent to inquire; the messenger returned with news of some importance, for, as the audience twisted about and necks were craned in curiosity, a way was cleared through the crowd so that a Gascon soldier in travel-stained garments was permitted to walk directly up to the seats of the justices.

The halberds of the attendants sounded on the floor as the men halted, one on each side of the soldier; but there also sounded, during the entrance of the group, what resembled the butt of a third halberd, but which was, remarkably enough, a wooden leg worn by the Gascon soldier.

The judges surveyed the newcomer. He was sunburned, and bearded, but through the beard the shape of the high, cleft chin was easily discernible. His left eyebrow was scarred; and there was a trace of an old ulcer on one cheek. He returned the scrutiny of the judges of Toulouse with eyes which were arrogant, gray and cold.

"Body of God," said one of the justices, sinking back in his seat in something not unlike despair, "this is either Martin Guerre or the devil," and he gave an order to the attendants to put the newcomer under arrest.

After brief deliberation among the judges, the order was also given to remove the accused man to an adjoining chamber and to close the doors against further entrance. This done, the weary justices proceeded to examine the soldier with the wooden leg.

"I am without any doubt Martin Guerre," said the soldier. "I lost my leg before St. Quentin in the year fifty-seven. I am the father of Sanxi Guerre, and of no other children."

To all the questions which had previously been put to the accused man, the soldier was able to reply with reasonable accuracy. Once or twice his answers were at variance with those of Bertrande to the same question, now and again he hesitated before answering, but in the main he showed a knowledge of the affairs of Martin Guerre which might well have justified his claim to be that man. He also manifested an unusual knowledge of the career of Arnaud du Tilh. This was interesting, for the accused man had known nothing at all of the affairs of du Tilh; he had heard rumors of his existence—that was all. But the newcomer seemed no better informed concerning the affairs of Martin Guerre than the accused had seemed. At the end of an hour the judges were no nearer a decision than they had been early that morning.

There remained a final test, however. The prisoner was summoned and made to stand face to face with the one-legged soldier. Then, one by one, the relatives of the two men were called, and asked to make their choice.

Carbon Bareau, the first of the relatives of du Tilh to be called, stared for a moment with great surprise at the soldier, then, turning without any hesitation at all, laid his hand on the shoulder of the prisoner and said:

"Gentlemen, this is my nephew."

The brothers of Arnaud, confronted by the two men so extraordinarily similar, hesitated, and then, turning from the prisoner as from the soldier, besought the court to excuse them from bearing witness. The court, with a humanity rare in that century, dismissed them. They had in their request testified more than they realized.

When the youngest sister of Martin Guerre was admitted, she lifted her hands to her forehead in a gesture full of amazement and distress, and then, without hesitation, flung herself upon the breast of the soldier with the wooden leg and burst into tears. One by one the other relatives of Martin Guerre, being admitted, stared with surprise from the soldier to the prisoner and back again, and confessed with many apologies and protestations of sorrow at their mistake that the soldier with one leg was undeniably Martin Guerre, who had been so long away.

It was remarkable that while Martin Guerre received this succession of tearful recognitions with a consistent, stern reserve, Arnaud du Tilh the prisoner, although growing perceptibly graver, lost none of his calm air of assurance and none of his dignity.

Meanwhile the judges, seeing which way the case had turned, sent to their hotel for Pierre Guerre and Bertrande de Rols. The day had been long. For these two lonely defenders of a cause it had seemed longer than a century. When the messenger came for them, they left the confinement of the inn and followed him through the still-confining streets with the intense fatalism of the defeated. The messenger had been instructed to tell them nothing, but rumor had preceded the messenger with the advice that the case had been decided against them. Pierre Guerre was admitted alone, and Bertrande, left in an ante-chamber with a guard, was clearly and sharply aware for the first time in that exhausting day of one thing, and that was that she could not return to Artigues as the wife of Arnaud du Tilh.

After a time the door to the courtroom opened, and she was admitted. She made her way through the crowd toward the space before the judges. Without looking up to see it, she yet felt the intense curiosity of all these unfamiliar faces bent upon her like a physical force. In the silence of the room the insatiable interest of the crowd beat upon her like a sultry wave. She reached the open space, and stopped. There she lifted her eyes at last and saw, standing beside Arnaud du Tilh the man whom she had loved and mourned as dead. She uttered a great cry and turned very pale. The pupils of her parti-colored eyes, the lucky eyes, expanded until the iris was almost lost. Then, reaching out her hands to Martin Guerre, she sank slowly to her knees before him. He did not make any motion toward her, so that, after a little time, she clasped her hands together and drew them toward her breast, and, recovering herself somewhat, said in a low voice:

"My dear lord and husband, at last you are returned. Pity me and forgive me, for my sin was occasioned only by my great desire for your presence, and surely, from the hour wherein I knew I was deceived, I have labored with all the strength of my soul to rid myself of the destroyer of my honor and my peace."

The tears began to run quietly down her face.

Martin Guerre did not reply immediately, and in the pause which followed, one of the justices, leaning forward, said to Bertrande:

"Madame, we have all been very happily delivered from a great error. Pray accept the profound apologies of this court which did not earlier sufficiently credit your story and your grief."

But Martin Guerre, when the justice had finished speaking, said to his wife with perfect coldness:

"Dry your tears, Madame. They cannot, and they ought not, move my pity. The example of my sisters and my uncle can be no excuse for you, Madame, who knew me better than any living soul. The error into which you plunged could only have been caused by willful blindness. You, and you only, Madame, are answerable for the dishonor which has befallen me."

Bertrande did not protest. Rising to her feet, she gazed steadily into the face of her husband and seemed there to see the countenance of the old Monsieur, the patriarch whose authority had been absolute over her youth and over that of the boy who had been her young husband. She recoiled from him a step or two in unconscious self-defense, and the movement brought her near to the author of her misfortunes, the actual Arnaud du Tilh.

In the silence which filled the courtroom at Martin's unexpected severity, a familiar voice close to her elbow pronounced gently:

"Madame, you wondered at the change which time and experience had worked in Martin Guerre, who from such sternness as this became the most indulgent of husbands. Can you not marvel now that the rogue, Arnaud du Tilh, for your beauty and grace, became for three long years an honest man?"

"Sirrah," answered Bertrande, "I marvel that you should speak to me, whose devotion has deprived me even of the pity of my husband. I once seemed to love you, it is true. I cannot now hate you sufficiently."

"I had thought to ask you to intercede for mercy for me," said Arnaud du Tilh.

"You had no mercy upon me, either upon body or upon soul," replied Bertrande.

"Then, Madame," said du Tilh, and there was at last neither arrogance nor levity in his voice, "I can but die by way of atonement."

Bertrande had turned to look at him as he spoke. She turned now from him towards her husband, and then, without speaking, moved slowly toward the door. The court did not detain her, and the crowd, in some awe, drew aside enough to let her pass without interruption. Bertrande did not see the crowd. Leaving the love which she had rejected because it was forbidden, and the love which had rejected her, she walked through a great emptiness to the door, and so on into the streets of Toulouse, knowing that the return of Martin Guerre would in no measure compensate for the death of Arnaud, but knowing herself at last free, in her bitter, solitary justice, of both passions and of both men.

Arnaud du Tilh, being confined in the prison at Artigues in the days which followed immediately upon the hearing at Toulouse, made a confession in which he stated that he had been tempted to the imposture by the frequency with which he had been mistaken for Martin Guerre. All that he knew of Martin's life and habits he had gleaned from Martin's friends, from his servants and from members of his family. He added that he had not originally intended to take Martin's place in his household, but had intended to stay only long enough to pick up a little silver or gold.

The court decreed that he had been convicted of the several crimes of imposture, falsehood, substitution of name and person, adultery, rape, sacrilege, plagiat, which is the detention of a person who properly belongs to another, and of larceny; and the court condemned him to do penance before the church of Artigues on his knees, in his shirt, with head and feet bare, a halter around his neck and a burning taper in his hand, asking pardon of God and of the king, of Martin Guerre and of Bertrande de Rols, his wife; the court then condemned him to be handed over to the common executioner, who should conduct him by the most public ways to the house of Martin Guerre, in front of which, upon a scaffold previously prepared, he should be hanged and his body burned. All his effects were forfeit to the crown. And this decree bears the date of September the twelfth, in the year 1560, in the city of Toulouse.

Of Martin Guerre nothing more is recorded, whether he returned to the wars or remained in Artigues, nor is there further record of Bertrande de Rols, his wife. But when hate and love have together exhausted the soul, the body seldom endures for long.